"So, Sophie....any ideas how we can spend our long afternoon?"

Was it just her, or had Lucas's voice dropped an octave? She swore she could feel it rumbling along her nerve endings. His eyelids dropped to half-mast as he stared at her mouth with intent.

He was going to kiss her. He was going to press his body against hers. His tongue was going to be in her mouth and his hands on her skin.

She reached out, her palms flattening against his chest. She was sure that she'd intended to push him away. Instead, she felt the hard curves of his pecs beneath her hands, and she clutched the fabric of his T-shirt, her arms flexing as she hauled him close so she could act on every one of the wild, illicit fantasies dancing across her mind.

It didn't matter that he was an ass, that he probably didn't have a sensitive or generous bone in his body. All she wanted was to get down and dirty and hot and sweaty with Lucas Grant.

Dear Reader,

I have to confess, this book was all about wish fulfillment... at least some of them.

The first was the food. Some people are addicted to smoking, alcohol, even gambling—for me it's food, and probably always will be. Not only did I salivate over the wonderful meals, I also got to explore the joys (?) of dieting by reversing the roles so that my hero had to skip the carbs and suck up the salad for a change. Ha! Take that, I thought every time I denied him bread and pasta and made him eat cottage cheese. See how you like it for a change...

The second was the luxurious Blue Mountain estate where Sophie and Lucas played out their sexy little games. This is a beautiful part of Australia, and what better way to share that beauty than with five-star accommodations?

But perhaps the best wish was seeing Lucas tamed by Sophie. He's a bad boy in the fashion of all those single movie stars whose exploits keep the tabloids in print, and it was gratifying when he fell for a woman who wasn't a model. I hope you enjoy reading this story as much as I did writing it.

If you'd like to chat, drop by the blog I share with several other Harlequin Blaze writers at www.loveisanexplodingcigar.com. Or you can contact me via the link to my Web site, www.sarahmayberryauthor.com. I love hearing from readers, so please don't be shy—it really makes my day.

Until next time,

Sarah Mayberry

BURNING UP
Sarah Mayberry

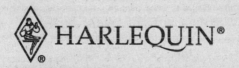

TORONTO • NEW YORK • LONDON
AMSTERDAM • PARIS • SYDNEY • HAMBURG
STOCKHOLM • ATHENS • TOKYO • MILAN • MADRID
PRAGUE • WARSAW • BUDAPEST • AUCKLAND

ISBN-13: 978-0-373-79384-6
ISBN-10: 0-373-79384-7

BURNING UP

www.eHarlequin.com

Printed in U.S.A.

ABOUT THE AUTHOR

Sarah Mayberry lives in Melbourne, Australia, with her partner, Chris, who is also a writer. When she's not writing a book, Sarah dabbles in TV drama as a scriptwriter and story editor. And when she's not doing either of the above, she likes to shop, read and sleep—not necessarily in that order.

Books by Sarah Mayberry

HARLEQUIN BLAZE

211—CAN'T GET ENOUGH
251—CRUISE CONTROL*
278—ANYTHING FOR YOU*
314—TAKE ON ME**
320—ALL OVER YOU**
326—HOT FOR HIM**

*It's All About Attitude
**Secret Lives of Daytime Divas

First up, a big thanks to Melbourne chef George Calombaris, the creator of the crazy, inspired meal that Sophie cooks in this book. I will never forget the first time I ate his food.

Also thanks to Chris, for holding my hand through rewrite hell, and to Sammas for first-chapter therapy via the Net. And, as always, thanks to Wanda, for letting me have the freedom to fix things. What would I do without you?

1

"COME ON IN, Lucas, the water's fine."

Lucas Grant took another slug of whiskey and squinted at the blonde bobbing in the hot tub at the end of his balcony. Until she'd spoken up, he hadn't realized anyone had stayed behind when the last guests had stumbled out the door of his Sydney harborside mansion a few minutes earlier.

He'd forgotten this one's name. Candy? Cindy? Something with a C, he was pretty sure. She was lying back in the water, arms spread wide on the rim behind her, her hair tousled, her eyes heavy-lidded.

A slow grin tugged at the corners of his mouth as he registered the trail of clothing she'd left on the way to the tub—a slinky little dress and the few scraps of Lycra and lace she'd obviously been wearing underneath.

Lucas moved toward her, tumbler held loosely in one hand.

"This is a surprise," he said, even though it wasn't.

Ever since he'd scored a role in a break-out movie back in his early twenties, his life had been full of moments like these. Blondes in hot tubs, brunettes waiting in his hotel room, redheads lingering outside the sound stage. Fame was the most powerful aphrodisiac known to mankind.

Or should that be womankind?

Whatever. The important thing was that despite the impressive quantity of alcohol he'd managed to guzzle this evening, his body was more than willing to take advantage of what was being so freely and generously offered.

As he stepped up onto the wood deck surrounding the tub, Candy-Cindy rose up out of the water, revealing her toned, tanned, cosmetically enhanced body to him in all its glory. He squelched the minor disappointment he felt at the realization that her generous twin endowments were man-made—did it really matter, at the end of the day?—and admired the way the water slicked down her slim, long-legged body.

"I hope you don't mind…?" she asked, eyes wide. Tough to pull off the whole innocent Bambi routine when she was standing there naked and perky, but she gave it a shot anyway and he awarded her full points for trying.

His grin widened. "Baby, you are just what the doctor ordered," he said.

Setting his glass on the tub surround, he pulled her close, one hand sliding down to cup a perfectly sculpted ass cheek, the other honing in on one of her twin assets. She closed her eyes as he moved in for a kiss, her lips opening beneath his with practiced ease. She tasted of wine, and her body was hot and firm against his. Moaning a little in the back of her throat, she slid a hand between their bodies and grabbed his hard-on through the denim of his jeans.

"You are not going to freakin' believe this," a male voice said behind them.

Candy-Cindy gave a little gasp of surprise and broke away from Lucas, covering herself with her hands. Lucas closed his eyes in frustration and swore loudly. Not for the first time, he regretted the necessity for his agent-cum-manager, Derek Lambert, to have a key to his house.

"Derek, mate, I'm a little busy, in case you hadn't noticed," he said brusquely, turning to frown at Derek.

True to character, Derek was completely unfazed. It didn't matter to him that it was late on a Saturday night. Deal making was a twenty-four-hour job where he was concerned.

"Check it out. Completely unauthorized. We're lucky we've had any forewarning at all before it hit the shelves."

For the first time Lucas registered the paperback book his manager was brandishing—and, more importantly, his own image staring at him from the front cover. Big red letters scrawled across the bottom of the photograph—*The Man Behind the Golden Eyes: An Unauthorized Biography of Lucas Grant.*

Lucas swore again and reached for the book.

"What the hell…? How did we not know about this?" he asked.

"Small publishing house and a sneaky little rat of a muckraking journalist. The only reason we know about it now is because someone owed me a favor."

Derek's gaze shifted to Candy-Cindy, who had sunk back into the water, her ears almost visibly flapping as she took in their conversation.

"Hey. I'm Derek. Pleased to meet you," Derek said,

smoothing a hand down the front of his custom-made navy pinstriped suit as he sat on the tub surround. "I'm Lucas's manager."

"I'm Camilla. Pleased to meet you." Lucas didn't need to look at her to know she was pouting and throwing her shoulders back. Derek might be short, tubby and barely hanging on to the last of his dark hair, but he oozed power and connections. No doubt Camilla wanted to be an actress or a model or maybe just plain old famous, and Derek was never averse to playing the you-scratch-my-back-I'll-scratch-yours game.

Returning his attention to the book, Lucas noted the crappy paper, the close-set print, the shoddy binding.

"This is a piece of shit," he said dismissively, ready to toss it to one side. "No one's going to read it."

"I don't care. We're both going over the damn thing with a fine-tooth comb. If there's a single factual inaccuracy in there, we can get a court order and kill this thing right off the bat. If there's anything that burns me up, it's people squeezing a buck out of you without going through me. We're going to make these assholes pay."

"Fine. I'll take a look at it in the morning," Lucas said, his thoughts reverting to Camilla as she stretched a long leg out of the water.

"We need to move quickly if we're going to stop this thing. I'll hang around while you take a look at it tonight," Derek said, his own gaze also glued to Camilla's limbs.

"I have other plans," Lucas pointed out.

"She'll wait. Won't you, sweetheart?" Derek asked.

Camilla nodded eagerly. "Sure. I'll just amuse myself out here."

Derek grinned at the suggestive note in her voice. "I'm sure you will. I'm sure you're a very resourceful woman."

Lucas shot his manager a look. "Easy, tiger." Sometimes Derek got off on the whole showbiz lifestyle thing a little too much for Lucas's personal comfort.

"I don't mind," Camilla said, arching her back so that her breasts broke the surface of the water.

Predictably, Derek's eyes honed in on them like heat-seeking missiles.

Suddenly, Lucas felt an overwhelming need to be done with this situation. Camilla's avid eagerness, Derek's willingness to exploit her, even Lucas's own recent urge to take what was offered and damn the consequences—suddenly it all seemed a little seedy and a lot desperate. The whiskey taste in his mouth soured and he felt bone-weary and more than ready to be alone.

"You know what? Maybe I *should* take care of this tonight and we can catch up another time," he said, turning to Camilla.

She started to pout, but the night was over for him. He wanted—needed—some space.

"I can take Camilla home, if you like," Derek said before Lucas could speak again.

There was a moment where the blatant calculation behind Camilla's gaze was there for all to see as she weighed up her options. Then she smiled.

"Okay. That sounds fun," she said.

Five minutes later Camilla and Derek were gone and Lucas had parked his butt on a balcony lounger and opened the first chapter of the book. Admittedly he was half-cut, but he wasn't expecting to be mentally challenged by what was sure to be a bunch of cobbled-together press releases and gossip. He'd skim through the usual bullshit about his early training at the National Institute for the Dramatic Arts in Sydney, his seminal roles in iconic Australian movies, and his fast-track to international fame, then he'd leave a reassuring message on Derek's phone and call it a night.

Instead, he read the opening few paragraphs and went rigid with tension.

Famous throughout the world, Lucas Grant's million-dollar smile and golden eyes are the trade-marks that have made him one of the highest-grossing movie stars in Hollywood today. Despite a high-profile social life that frequently titillates the mass media, Grant refuses to give personal interviews and is fiercely private about his past, leaving legions of fans to guess at what drives the world's most famous playboy.

With the publication of this book, the guessing games are over. This reporter has uncovered sensational information about Lucas Grant's background—his childhood abandonment, the many state homes he lived in while the government tried to find a foster placement for this troubled young boy and the hurdles Grant has had to conquer in order to become the man he is today.

Lucas tore through the pages, scanning one after the other after the other. It was all there, everything he'd never spoken about, everything that belonged firmly in the past.

Throwing the book to one side, he shot to his feet on a surge of adrenaline. He wanted to hit someone, but there was no one handy. Certainly not the sneaky little bastard who'd unearthed all of his darkest secrets.

Shit.

Shit.

Shit.

He reached for the phone to call Derek and demand he do everything in his power to stop publication. No way was Lucas going to be the object of pity at the hands of some bottom-feeding parasite attempting to cash in.

But common sense stilled Lucas's hand on the touch pad. The only way they could stop this thing from going public was to prove it was slanderous and inaccurate. And so far, it had proved to be highly, painfully accurate. Which meant there was no way they could stop it.

Pacing, he ran a hand through his dark hair, trying to think past the alcohol haze.

The rules of public relations were pretty clear in situations like this. He either tried to beat them to the punch by outing himself and owning his history by telling it his way. Or he ignored the book's existence and hoped it died a quiet, unread death.

Just the thought of following through with option one made every muscle in his body rigid.

It was never going to happen. Ever.

Which left him with option two: sit by and hope that the book sank without a trace into the sea of ink released worldwide every month.

He swore again, hating the sense of powerlessness

rocketing through him. A long time ago he'd made a deal with the public in exchange for their adoration and movie-viewing dollars—he'd drop slightly naughty sound bites, he'd frequent the party scene, he'd exchange gorgeous women weekly, he'd live large and wild while allowing it all to be photographed for the masses' consumption, But that agreement did *not* include an all-areas access pass into his life. Not by a long shot. Some things nobody needed to know.

Needing to vent his rage, he kicked the lounger, sending it sliding along the tiles until it slammed into a potted palm. Still unsatisfied, he searched for something else to knock around and his gaze fell on the book.

Teeth bared in a snarl, he strode toward it, intent on booting it with all his might. Pulling his left leg back, he pushed off on his right, swinging forward in a hard, powerful kick full of fury and frustration. Then his right foot slipped and he realized too late that Camilla's thong was underneath.

Arms wheeling, he skidded, his left leg propelling him forward with unstoppable momentum. His foot missed the book and instead he collided—hard—into the tempered-glass railing.

It gave with a resounding smash—as did what felt like every muscle and bone in his lower leg.

Lying on his back, a world of pain shooting up his leg, Lucas threw back his head and howled into the night sky.

SOPHIE GALLAGHER juggled shopping bags from one hand to the other as she searched for her house keys, finally finding them in the side pocket of her purse.

"Here, let me take those," her best friend, Becky Kincaid, offered, holding out a hand for the bags.

"Thanks, but I'm all right," Sophie assured her as they entered the apartment she shared with her fiancé, Brandon.

"Brandon is going to lose it when he sees you in that bustier and stockings," Becky said as they dumped their parcels on the couch.

"Here's hoping," Sophie said, crossing both her fingers.

That had been the whole purpose of their shopping expedition, after all—finding something to help remind Brandon that, once upon a time, they used to have sex, rather than roll into bed each night and fall asleep after a perfunctory hug and kiss.

She blamed their inactivity on the fact that, as well as living together, they both worked in his family's restaurant, Sorrentino's—her has head chef, him as host. Sexual mystery and surprise went out the window when two people spent most of every day in each other's company. Plus there was the fact that they'd been together for nearly fourteen years now. No wonder they needed a jump-start.

"He'd have to be blind not to react to that sexy little number," Becky said loyally. "Although I still think you should have tried on that hot-pink one with the embroidery and the little transparent bits."

Sophie shrugged. "I would have felt like such an impostor. As it is all this black satin is going to be hard enough to pull off." Although she *had* been seriously tempted by the more daring lingerie. The bright color and the peek-a-boo panels had practically screamed wild, wanton woman.

Which was exactly why she hadn't done more than admire it from a distance. She wasn't remotely wild or wanton. She was reliable, calm, practical, dependable—pretty much the polar opposite of wild and wanton.

Upending one of the bags and shaking the contents out, Sophie blinked as an image from the past rushed her. Her older sister tipping another bag out onto the bed in their shared bedroom and a sea of color tumbling out—pink and aqua and purple and green. Thongs and push-up bras, a pair of tap pants and a sexy see-through bra all in silk and satin and lace. And all of it shoplifted, of course, courtesy of crazy, impetuous Carrie's quick fingers. She had always been attracted to danger and fun.

Sophie ran a hand over the smooth, cool satin of the simple bustier she'd chosen today. Without a doubt, Carrie would have chosen the hot-pink one, and she would have worn it with sass and verve....

"You okay?" Becky asked, nudging Sophie with an elbow.

Sophie snapped out of her reverie, shaking off the old sadness.

"Sure."

Glancing up, Sophie caught sight of the wall clock and nearly had a heart attack.

"Damn. He's going to be home in twenty minutes," she said.

"Into the shower. Quick. I'll put this stuff on your bed and get the champagne ready," Becky ordered.

Sophie hugged her friend impulsively. "Has anyone ever told you you'd make a great pimp?" she said.

"All the time. Why do you think I became a lawyer?" Becky said, poker-faced. "Now go make yourself irresistible."

Sophie hustled into the bathroom, shucking her clothes in record time and stepping under the water before it even had a chance to warm up.

As she reached for the soap, she made a mental note to take Becky out for dinner or to buy her a thank-you gift for all her support. Sophie had never been big on talking about sex—perhaps because she and Brandon had been together since high school. They'd been each other's first lovers, and there had never been anyone else for either of them. So it had taken a while for her to confide in her friend about such an intensely personal and private matter. Fortunately, Becky had proved to be a veritable treasure trove of information, with advice on everything from the best place to buy saucy lingerie to which books to read for bedroom advice.

"Soph, I'm going to skedaddle. You okay to take it from here on your own?" Becky called around the door. Sophie didn't need to see her friend's face to know she was smiling.

"Ah, yeah. I think I know what to do next," Sophie said, tongue-in-cheek.

"Good *lu-uck!*" Becky singsonged on her way out the door.

Her mind on the time, Sophie turned the water off and scrambled out. Whisking a towel over herself, she walked naked and still damp into the bedroom and began to cinch herself into the bustier. It was an absolute bitch putting the stupid thing on backward and twisting it the right way around, but she figured the end result was more than worth it.

Making short work of rolling on black silk stockings, Sophie slid her feet into a pair of stiletto heels. She was short, her figure more Rubenesque than anorexic, but the high cut of her new panties and the dark stockings and high heels worked wonders. Satisfied with what she saw in the full-length mirror inside her closet door, she reached for her makeup bag. She'd finished lining her big brown eyes with smoky-kohl and was just dabbing on mascara when the phone rang. Groaning with frustration, she grabbed it and tried to do her other eye with the phone wedged between her shoulder and her ear.

"Hello?"

"Sophie, it's Julie Jenkins calling," a cultured voice said, and Sophie recognized one of the restaurant's wealthiest patrons.

While she'd catered private functions for Julie a few times in the past, the other woman had never called her at home before. Switching gears, Sophie endeavored to sound professional even though she was acutely aware that she was dressed like a refugee from *The Rocky Horror Picture Show.*

"Julie. How are you?"

"Very well, thank you. Sophie, I'm calling to ask a favor. I need someone to act as private chef on my Blue Mountains estate for the next four weeks. An old friend of mine is recuperating from an injury. Would you be interested?"

Sophie frowned and put down the mascara wand.

"I'm sorry, but there's no way I could take time off from Sorrentino's at such short notice," she explained.

"What if I told you your client would be Lucas Grant?" Julie asked hopefully.

Sophie's eyebrows shot up. Lucas Grant was Brandon's absolute favorite actor. Personally, while she admired his acting, she found his rampant bad-boy persona ridiculous. The man was in his thirties, when was he going to stop partying and grow up?

"Tempted?" Julie asked, clearly hoping Sophie would change her mind.

"Sorry, there really is no way I could get the time off," Sophie repeated.

"Pity. The money's good, and you were the first person I thought of," Julie said. "You know how John and I love your cooking."

"Thanks, Julie. And thanks for thinking of me. I only wish I could help you out," Sophie said.

"Not a problem. And just so you know, Sophie, no one who knows anything about food paid a bit of attention to that foolish review last month. Sorrentino's will always be our first choice when dining out," Julie said.

They ended the call after another few minutes of small talk. But instead of diving back into her makeup bag, Sophie stared sightlessly at her hands, brooding once again about the restaurant review that had rocked her world last month.

She hadn't even known they were being reviewed. When the photographer made contact to take shots of the dining room, explaining the reviewer had already been in for his meal, she'd felt slightly cheated. She liked to put her best foot forward when she knew a foodie was expected. Still, she hadn't been too worried. Sorrentino's had an excellent reputation and she'd received a strong recommendation from the same magazine five years ago.

Not so this time. She still remembered the words by heart. How could she not? They were etched into her pride.

> On our last visit five years ago, Sophie Gallagher of Sorrentino's in Surry Hills seemed set to become one of the shining lights of the Australian restaurant world. But it seems time has stood still in Sorrentino's kitchen. On our return, we found the menu little changed, a disappointing discovery when dining in Sydney has taken some huge and exciting leaps forward in recent years. All was done well, but the choices on offer were safe, conservative, unadventurous. One can only guess that Ms. Gallagher has settled into a premature middle age.

Every time she thought of that last line, she wanted to spit. Smug bastard, passing judgment on her through her menu. She'd ranted and raved for days after the magazine came out, but fortunately the restaurant's bookings had remained solid and Brandon and his parents had been more than ready to slough the whole thing off and forget it.

Probably good advice, but the review continued to niggle at Sophie, especially when people mentioned it to her—even well-intentioned people like Julie. A dozen times over the past five years she'd experimented with new dishes for the menu, testing new ideas and combinations. But always she returned to the understanding that Sorrentino's was a family restaurant—an elegant, neighborhood place where husbands took their wives for anniversaries and their children for birthday celebrations. The menu she'd created five years ago suited their clientele admirably, as the restaurant's success attested. Why rock the boat?

The sound of a key in the front door shook Sophie out of her brooding and had her shooting to her feet. She'd only mascaraed one eye, and her short, pixie-cut auburn hair was clinging damply to her skull. Ruffling it with her fingertips, she snatched at a lipstick and smoothed on some color just as the door to the bedroom swung open and Brandon entered.

It was Sunday, and they had exactly three hours before either of them was due at the restaurant for the night. They had champagne, black satin and sexy music—everything they needed for a little horizontal play. Throwing her shoulders back, Sophie struck what she hoped was a sexy pose.

"Surprise!" she said, giving him her best come-hither look.

Brandon froze. His gaze ran up and down her body. Then his shoulders slumped and he closed his eyes for a long, long beat.

When he opened them, the look in his eyes made her stomach dip with fear.

"Sophie, we need to talk," he said.

2

TWO HOURS LATER, Sophie pulled into the darkened driveway of Julie Jenkins's Blue Mountains estate west of Sydney. Behind her on the backseat of her rusty Volkswagen Beetle was a box containing a jumble of cookbooks, her recipe folder, her knife roll and, for some absurd reason, a can opener. She'd thrown it all together haphazardly when what Brandon had told her had sunk in.

They were over. Finished. Fourteen years gone, just like that.

Hot tears burned at the backs of Sophie's eyes as she wound her way up a long driveway, and she knuckled them away and swallowed noisily.

He hadn't even wanted to talk. That was the thing that hurt the most. He'd presented her with a fait accompli.

"Sophie, I can't do this anymore," he'd said. "I'm sick of hoping things will change. I'm sick of lying in bed night after night like an old married couple. I don't want to get to forty and look back and wonder where my life has gone."

"I know we've been in a rut lately," she'd said, and he'd laughed—a sharp, hard, angry laugh.

"A rut? Jesus, Sophie, we're in the Grand freaking Canyon."

"So we talk. We do something about it. What do you think this afternoon is all about?"

Brandon had sat on the end of the bed and put his head in his hands. "Sophie, a bunch of satin is not going to patch over our problems. It's time to face the facts— we passed our use-by date years ago."

That had made her legs go weak and she'd been forced to sit beside him.

"That's so not true," she'd said. "We still love each other. We're best friends. We just need to take time to rediscover each other again."

"We love each other, but we're not *in* love, Sophie. We haven't been for a long time."

"Speak for yourself."

Then he'd sucker-punched her. "I want to sleep with other women."

She'd gasped. It was a slap in the face the way he'd said it so abruptly.

"I'm sorry, but it's true. Don't you ever wonder what it would be like with someone else?" he'd asked, searching her face with his eyes.

"No. No, I don't."

He'd nodded then. "I suppose that's probably true. You like things to stay the same, I know that. You like your routines, and knowing what's going to happen next. Well, I can't do it anymore. I feel like I'm suffocating."

He'd started packing a suitcase then, and she'd been frozen with shock as she tried to comprehend what was happening.

"You'll thank me, you'll see. You just need a push to make you get out there and spread your wings. We've been hiding with each other for too long, Soph."

She'd been about to throw herself at his feet and beg him to talk more, to at least give them a chance to try to make things work. But the patronizing, all-knowing, parental tone of his words had made her bristle. And she'd done the first thing that had sprung to mind— picked up the phone and called Julie Jenkins.

And now she was pulling up outside a huge, two-story house—mansion, really—about to embark on four weeks of pandering to one of the world's most indulged men.

Once again tears threatened, but Sophie refused to cry. She was angry, not sad, she told herself. The things Brandon had said to her, about her… She felt as though he'd been kidnapped by pod people and replaced with an alien. How could he have been thinking and feeling that way and she never had a clue?

For a moment she felt overwhelmed.

She was single. It was almost incomprehensible. She'd been with Brandon since she was sixteen years old, but now, suddenly, at thirty, she was single. Alone. Adrift. All her plans, all her dreams, gone in the time it had taken Brandon to pack his suitcase.

For a moment she gave in to the confusion and leaned forward, resting her forehead against the steering wheel. She had no idea what was going to happen tomorrow, or the day after that. She had no idea where she'd be in a month's time, a year's time.

A huge gulf of fear seemed to yawn at her feet.

You like your routines and knowing what's going to happen next.

Brandon's words tickled at the edges of her mind and she sat up straight and thumped the steering wheel with her fist.

Why did she feel so defensive about what he'd said? What was wrong with liking routines? With enjoying the known, the secure?

"Nothing," she said out loud.

Brandon was the one who'd given up on them. He was the one with doubts, urges, unfulfilled desires. This was not about her.

Her jaw set, Sophie swung the door open. Tomorrow morning, Lucas Grant was arriving for a four-week recuperation spell after injuring himself on set, according to Julia Jenkins. Sophie had tonight to look over the strict diet she'd been sent and familiarize herself with the kitchen.

Both tasks that she could handle with one hand tied behind her back, despite what Brandon had said about her.

"Bastard," she said under her breath. It felt better to be angry. If she wasn't angry, she had the feeling she was going to be very, very sad. And she wasn't ready to deal with that yet.

THE FOLLOWING MORNING, Lucas threw down his bag and looked around. He'd known the Jenkinses for a long time—ever since John had taught him drama at NIDA, in fact—but he'd never realized quite how loaded they were until now. The Blue Mountains "house" that Julie had offered him for his recovery was, in fact, a sprawl-

ing estate, complete with heated in-ground pool, caretaker's lodge and a spectacular seven-bedroom main
house with high, arched ceilings, imported stone floors
and every modern convenience. If he didn't already own
three houses of his own—L.A., New York, Sydney—
he'd almost be envious.

He guessed if he had to be stuck on crutches, there
were worse places to be, and not many better.

Frowning, he glanced down at the bulge his newly
acquired knee brace made beneath his jeans. He'd torn his
ankle ligaments, as well as the medial ligament in his
knee. The whole of his foot was bruised and slightly
swollen, although it was hard to tell since most of it was
hidden by removable neoprene braces, designed to hold
his ankle and knee in the correct position while his tendons
healed. The doctor had told him it was a miracle that he
hadn't broken anything, considering what had happened.

It had been two days since the accident, and his leg
still hurt like hell. Fortunately, they'd given him some
serious Tyrannosaurus-Rex-strength painkillers—as
well as strict instructions to take it easy for at least four
weeks. Which was why Derek had insisted he take Julie
up on the offer of her mountain hideaway. Lucas had a
film scheduled to begin shooting next week, and the
whole production had been delayed to allow him time
to recover. The studio had insurance to cover this sort
of situation, but Lucas wasn't exactly the golden-haired
boy right now.

He shrugged the thought off as he dropped his crutches
beside the bed and flopped backward onto the king-size
mattress. Four weeks wasn't going to kill anyone—him

or the studio. Yeah, he'd stuffed up a little. But it wasn't as though he'd meant to slip and collide with the balcony railing. If it hadn't been for that biography…

Crossing his arms behind his head, Lucas stared at the ceiling. It was bloody quiet up here in the mountains. No hum of traffic, no people moving around, no chatter of voices in distant rooms. The only sound he could hear was the faint chirrup of birds in the gum trees outside.

Peaceful. Huh.

After about five minutes of peaceful, he started to get a little twitchy. He wasn't used to having time on his hands. Usually he spent at least two hours a day training—weights, running, yoga for flexibility. If he wasn't actually shooting a film, he usually had costume fittings, makeup tests, meetings with studios, meetings with Derek or meetings with anyone else who wanted a piece of him, not to mention all the promotional commitments for new releases such as interviews and photo shoots. At night, there were premieres, openings and parties to attend…. His cup runneth over, as it were. Just the way he liked it.

Except for the next four weeks. Frowning, Lucas had a sudden vision of how the next month was going to pan out—lots of birds tweeting and him lying around like this wishing he was elsewhere. In his mind, time slowed to a turtle's crawl, days stretched into weeks, weeks into months, months into—

Shit. Maybe coming up here alone was a bad idea. In the hospital, doped to the eyeballs and copping flack from the studio and Derek, a little peace and quiet had seemed extremely desirable.

But not this much peace and quiet.

Sliding his cell phone from his pocket, Lucas scrolled through his address book and punched speed dial. The phone rang once before a familiar voice picked up.

"David, mate, how are you?" he asked.

"Lucas. You're still alive, are you? Heard you got drunk and fell off a balcony or something," David Gracie said, laughing down the line.

Lucas and David had trained together at NIDA, and after a slow start David was now knocking back offers to appear in multimillion-dollar films, his star firmly on the rise.

"A slight exaggeration. Just got a dodgy knee for a few weeks," Lucas explained lightly. The joys of being famous—everyone knew his business about two seconds after he did. "I've got a few weeks off, anyway, and I was wondering whether you wanted to grab a few warm bodies and come hang in the Blue Mountains?"

"Mate, I'd love to, but I'm about to head out to L.A. Maybe another time, yeah?"

"Sure, man. Absolutely."

Ending the call, Lucas scanned his address book for another likely suspect.

"Hey, Mikey, how you doin'?" he asked as another acting buddy picked up.

But Mikey was in the middle of a theatrical season at the Opera House playing King Lear. In fact, it seemed all his old friends were tied up with something over the next few weeks. Some of them had day jobs now, having given up acting for something more reliable. Others had families, God forbid. No one was free to come play in the mountains. His thoughts flew to L.A., where there was always someone kicking around, ready to party. But there was no way any of his drinking buddies were about to jump on a plane and travel halfway around the world to stop him expiring from boredom.

"Damn." Giving up for the moment, Lucas tossed his phone to one side and rubbed the bridge of his nose. The painkillers were starting to wear off, and his ankle and knee were throbbing like bastards.

The real issue, however, was his isolation. How the hell was he going to stay sane for four whole weeks of *nothing?*

Vaguely it occurred to him that there was something faintly pathetic about being so reliant on other people and stimuli to help him get by. What kind of man couldn't stand a few hours of his own company, let alone a few weeks? Maybe he ought to tough it out up here to prove to himself that he could. Some early nights, a bit of clean living. Maybe it would even do him good.

Tension crawled up his back and into his shoulders at the very thought.

"Stuff it."

Grabbing his phone again, he rang Derek, rolling his eyes when it went through to voice mail. Typical, the one time he actually wanted to talk to the guy.

"Listen. This stupid mountain idyll thing was a big mistake," he told Derek's voice mail. "Call me back and we'll make other plans."

Ending the call, he reached for the side pocket on his suitcase and found the painkillers he'd been prescribed.

Tossing back a couple, he gritted his teeth until the world began to blur at the edges a little.

"That's more like it," he muttered to himself.

Levering himself up on his elbows, he glanced out the window and spotted his first pleasant surprise of the day—out on the balcony stood a big, kick-ass telescope.

"All right."

Grabbing his crutches, he lumbered to the French doors that opened onto the balcony and stepped outside. He was greeted with a gust of hot, eucalyptus-tinged air, the warmth actually welcome after the air-conditioned house.

He'd always had a thing for telescopes, and he'd been meaning to buy one of his own for years. Somehow, though, he never seemed to spend enough time in any of his three homes to get around to investing in one.

The lens and eyepiece were protected by rubber caps, and he tugged them loose and lowered his head to the eyepiece. The telescope was trained down and to the right of the pool, and at first he saw nothing but blurry shapes and indistinct light and shadow.

It took him a moment to locate the right dials, but soon Lucas was twisting knobs experimentally—until the image in front of his eyes shifted abruptly into sharp focus.

"Holy hell!" he said, his head jerking back from the telescope in surprise.

He stared blankly at the sky for a short beat, then grinned widely and lowered his head to the telescope again to make sure that his eyes had not been deceiving him.

Framed perfectly between the not-completely-lowered edge of a Venetian blind and the windowsill of the caretaker's lodge were the prettiest, plumpest, most delicious-looking breasts he'd seen in a long time. Full, creamy-white, with soft pink nipples that seemed to be sitting up and begging for his attention, they looked silky-smooth and very, very edible.

The owner of the breasts was moving around, shifting things. A book. A folded piece of clothing. She was wearing a fluffy towel cinched around her waist, and he eyed the torso beneath the breasts, trying to imagine what the rest of her body might be like. Long legs? Peachy ass? And did she wax? Or was there a thatch of curls between her thighs?

"Damn it," Lucas said in frustration, then he sucked in a breath as the woman loosened the towel and let it fall to the ground.

"Oh, baby."

His gaze roamed over her curvy, pert, juicy-looking butt, lingering on the two enticing dimples nestled in the small of her back.

Registering the tightness in his jeans, Lucas glanced down. He was as hard as a rock, his boner straining against his fly. At the sight he suddenly understood what he was doing—spying on some unknown, unaware woman like a pervert. Or, at best, a horny teenager. Neither category he was eager to qualify for. He might be a hard-drinking, womanizing party animal, but he wasn't desperate.

Taking one last, lingering look at the breasts and an ass that would surely haunt him for days, Lucas forced himself to step back from the telescope.

Who was she? That was the burning question. The

caretaker? Some kind of domestic staff? A vague memory floated to the top of his brain—Julie explaining that she'd arranged for a local chef to take care of his meals for the duration of his stay.

So, she was the chef. *Interesting.*

Lucas grinned to himself. Suddenly he had something to do. Meet the chef. Check out the rest of her hot little body. And maybe he could find a better way to kill time than staring at the ceiling and contemplating his own navel. Maybe he could contemplate *her* navel… among other things.

His grin got broader. He had a project.

Excellent.

3

SOPHIE PULLED ON underwear and dressed in a pair of black yoga pants and a stretchy, striped tank top. She'd had a crappy night's sleep, tossing and turning, thinking belatedly of clever, pithy things she should have said to Brandon rather than stand mutely by while he told her how it was going to be.

Not that she would have wanted things to turn out any differently, not now that he'd made his true feelings so abundantly clear. A whole night's reflection had brought her that much clarity, at least.

He wanted to have sex with other women.

He wanted to be free.

He thought she was staid and boring and bound by routine.

He really was a bastard. It was the perfect word to describe a man who could throw away fourteen years without even pausing to take a breath and discuss it properly. It wasn't as though he'd even given her a chance to change, or fired off any warning shots to indicate their relationship was about to implode. He'd just made a decision and acted on it, without thinking of her at all.

Suddenly she recalled a night about six months ago when Brandon had shot to his feet and headed for the door when she'd suggested they watch *There's Something About Mary* again. It was one of her favorite movies, and he'd always enjoyed it. But that night he'd launched himself out the door without a word, returning twenty minutes later with a selection of new-release DVDs from the video store.

Had that been her early warning signal?

Sophie frowned as she remembered that she'd never asked him why he'd done that.

Maybe because she hadn't wanted to know the answer?

Sophie shook her head, rejecting the thought and the memory. She had work to do. Besides, did any of it matter when Brandon had pulled the pin on their relationship for good? Going over and over every little detail wasn't going to change anything.

Padding barefoot across the polished floor of the small but luxuriously appointed cottage, Sophie made her way to the kitchen to prepare her first meal for her star client, determined to resolutely keep her thoughts on the here and now.

She'd heard a voice—presumably talking on a cell phone—by the pool earlier and guessed that Mr. Grant had arrived. She'd been given a schedule to follow for his meals, as well as his very strict diet plan. It wouldn't take her long to whip up the steamed chicken, green vegetable and cottage cheese salad that was allocated for his first meal. Frankly, a grade-school kid could probably throw the meal together, it was so basic. Not that she was complaining, given that this job had provided her the perfect escape hatch from her suddenly disastrous life.

Still, her chef's soul ached to add a dash of something to spice up the very bland salad—some toasted walnuts, a raspberry vinaigrette, maybe some wafer-thin slices of pear…none of which was included on the eating plan.

By the time that she'd prepared and presented the meal to her satisfaction—not that there was much she could do with such limited raw materials—it was ten minutes to the appointed lunchtime. Grabbing the plate, Sophie made her way past the pool, across the expansive terrace and through the wide sliding doors to the living room of the main house.

As she stepped over the threshold, a flutter of something that felt very much like nervousness danced around her belly. She stopped in her tracks, frowning.

Surely she wasn't *nervous* about meeting Lucas Grant for the first time? The man was an overgrown fourteen-year old who drank too much, partied too hard and went through women the way most people went through socks. Apart from the fact that he made a lot of money from performing what was essentially a very silly, pointless job, there was nothing special about him at all. In fact, compared to more worthy members of the human race—Mother Teresa, Nelson Mandela, to name a few—he was beneath contempt.

But still there was a little tickle of awareness about the fact that she would soon meet the man who had been voted World's Sexiest by *People* magazine three years in a row. The man who made women all over the world cross their legs and squirm in their seats. The man who reputedly had his perfect, rounded, muscular butt insured for over a million dollars.

Ridiculous. Pathetic. Sad.

But no matter how much she berated herself for being so shallow, it didn't make the feeling go away. As she crossed the vast living room and entered the kitchen, Sophie tried to shake her nerves off, assuring herself that no matter how Lucas Grant looked on the big screen, in reality he was probably short, obnoxious and hugely egotistical.

Rummaging in a drawer for cutlery, she dropped a fork as she told herself that he probably had big, fake, white teeth, a horrible orange tan from a bottle and a towering sense of self-entitlement. Crouching to pick the fork up, she smiled as she realized that she'd successfully killed the small buzz of anticipation humming through her body. He was just a man. Probably an idiot, to boot. And definitely nobody she'd care to meet under normal circumstances.

Too bad her sense of triumph was short-lived.

Bracing her legs to stand again, she registered the single, tanned, very masculine bare foot that had appeared in front of her, seemingly out of nowhere. Next to it was a second foot, this one encased in a bright blue neoprene and Velcro ankle brace. Bracketing the feet were the rubber tips and metal uprights of a pair of crutches.

Later she would think about how he'd snuck up on her so silently. The man was on crutches—what was he, a ninja or something?

For now, however she was too busy being swamped by a hot rush of pure, unadulterated, unexpected lust as her gaze traveled up the length of his jeans-clad legs, lingering first on the bulge around his left knee, then—for a much longer time—on the substantial and promising bulge in his crotch. Forcing herself to tear her fascinated gaze away, she completed the journey, her eyes trailing over his waistband and up, up, up over what seemed like a mile of tight-T-shirt-covered stomach and chest and shoulders to finally reach his tanned, chiseled, utterly gorgeous face. Finding herself staring into the most amazing pair of amber eyes she'd ever seen in her life, Sophie swallowed noisily and almost fell over backward. Those eyes were like hot caramel, she decided as she stared stupidly into them. Or really rich coffee cake. Or a rare, rare precious stone.

"Hi. I'm Lucas," he said, and she realized she was still crouched at his feet, her eyes practically bugging out of her head as she ogled him.

"Sophie. Gallagher. Sophie Gallagher is my name," she said, shooting upright abruptly.

He was…gorgeous. It was the only possible word that could be used to describe him. From the top of his artistically rumpled black hair to the tips of his big, bare, tanned toes, he was *All Man*. Hard, firm, golden-skinned man. Even being on crutches didn't dim his appeal one iota. If anything, it only increased it. He looked wounded. A hero back from the wars. A man in need of soothing.

"Great to meet you, Sophie," Lucas said, extending his hand.

She slid her hand into his automatically and her whole body shivered at the glide of his flesh on hers. She couldn't help wondering what his entire body would feel like beneath her hands—smooth and firm and warm, probably. He was so much bigger than her, too. She would definitely know she was with a man with him in her bed. The weight of him. His height, his breadth, his length.

Abruptly, Sophie realized that she was staring at Lucas Grant's crotch again. And that illicit heat was pooling between her thighs.

What the hell was wrong with her?

But she knew the answer: she was turned on. Her body had zoomed from zero to come-and-get-me in no seconds flat—merely because Lucas Grant had walked into the room, smiled at her and shaken her hand.

It was such a shocking bit of knowledge, Sophie didn't know what to do with it. She was twenty-four hours out of the only relationship she'd ever known. Brandon had just snapped her heart in two. She had no business being attracted to another man, especially one she'd just spent the last ten minutes denigrating for being shallow, feckless and immature.

She took a step backward, away from temptation and confusion. Feeling utterly overwhelmed, she glanced over her shoulder, looking for an escape route. The only door she could see led into the walk-in pantry. Good enough. Especially in an emergency. And this was definitely an emergency.

"If you're after your lunch, I'll bring it to you in a few minutes," she said, backing toward the pantry.

"There's no rush," he said easily.

She felt the heat of his gaze flicking up and down her body, and her breasts tingled with awareness.

Good God.

Her fingers found the cool wood of the pantry door with relief.

"I have to, um, take care of something," she said, then she turned and stepped into the pantry.

Standing in the relative dark surrounded by shelves of dry goods, she pressed a hand to her belly, aware of the steady pulse of her elevated heartbeat thrumming beneath her palm. Her breath sounded loud and fast in the confined space and she blinked several times, trying to work out what the hell was going on with her.

This had to be some kind of delayed reaction to what had happened with Brandon. She seized the explanation as if it were a lifeline. Of course that was what it was— some kind of weird expression of grief and loss. Her whole life had been turned upside down. She was bound to feel unsettled and…horny?

Closing her eyes, she made a helpless whimpering sound. Never in her life had she felt so out of control. So separated from her normal self. And she didn't like it—not one little bit.

She was nothing like he'd expected.

Lucas stared after the chef, a frown pleating his forehead. Those breasts, that ass—he'd automatically assumed they'd belong to a striking Amazonian beauty. A really flexible, nimble, nymphomaniac Amazonian beauty. The kind of woman who littered his world.

But Sophie Gallagher was short. A munchkin, in fact. Her head barely came to his shoulder. Her face was more round and friendly than angled and sexy. If he were casting a movie, she'd be a dead cert for the wacky best friend, but never the romantic lead. Big velvety-brown eyes, a snub nose, a full-lipped mouth and dark red hair in a whimsical pixie cut completed the picture.

Nope. Definitely not what he'd expected.

Not that she was unappealing. Far from. She was just…different from the kind of woman he normally dallied with.

Swiveling on his good foot, he hopped to the living room, since she didn't appear to be coming back from wherever she'd gone anytime soon. Pulling out a chair at the dining table, he sat and propped his crutches against the table.

Sophie. Her name was Sophie. He guessed she was in her late twenties, although it was hard to tell because she had very clear, youthful-looking skin. And though she might not be the kind of tall, leggy beauty he preferred, there was something earthy and warm about her. The more he thought about her, the more convinced he became that she was definitely worth exploring.

What the hell—it wasn't like he had any better options on his hands.

The slap of bare feet on the stone floor had him glancing up, and he followed her with his eyes as she walked toward him. She had a rather delicious little swing in her hips, he noted, that made her butt wiggle with each step. And she had that great rack.

Who knew? She might even start a whole new thing for short women with him.

He was about to flash her his most roguish, charming smile when he clocked the meal she was setting before him.

Thin, unappetizing slices of chicken. *Steamed* chicken, if he didn't miss his guess. A selection of green vegetables that looked even less appetizing than the chicken, if that were possible. And a white, amorphous blob of what he suspected was cottage cheese.

"What's this?" he asked, frowning. He was starving, and this crap was so not going to do the trick.

"Lunch. From your diet chart," she said, her eyes widening at his tone.

"My diet chart…?" he asked, before comprehension dawned.

Derek and the freaking studio.

He had his cell phone in his hands in no seconds flat.

SOPHIE TOOK A STEP BACK from the table as Lucas punched a button on his phone and waited impatiently for the call to connect. She couldn't take her eyes off him. He was just so very, very good-looking. Not perfect—that would have made him plastic and artificial and repellent. Instead, he had laugh lines around his mouth and a thin white scar bisecting the end of one eyebrow. Certainly flawed and human. And even more devastatingly attractive because of it.

This is what people must mean when they talk about star quality, she decided helplessly. Charisma, magnetism, charm—whatever it was called, he had it by the bucketful.

And she was trapped in the tractor beam of that charisma like an ant in honey. She couldn't seem to look away, despite having given herself a very firm talking to in the darkness of the pantry. Despite the fact, also, that he'd reacted as though she'd handed him a plateful of radioactive matter instead of a carefully prepared meal.

Help!

Any second now drool would spill out the side of her mouth and she'd start panting in earnest. Completely against her will. Completely against all her better instincts. All because he was tall.

And muscular.

And golden-skinned.

And he had those amazing eyes....

"You want to explain why the hell I'm on a diet?" he barked into the phone, his tone so sharp it made her jump.

Sophie blinked. Apparently when a person was famous, he didn't need to bother with social niceties like hellos and goodbyes. If that didn't quite break the spell his physical appeal had woven around her, his next words did.

"It's not like I've ever had a weight problem before, Derek," he said. "I don't need to have someone telling me what to eat day and night. Especially when it's tasteless crap I wouldn't feed a dog."

Tasteless crap? That he wouldn't feed a dog? That quickly, Sophie snapped out of her lust-induced fog.

All her former disdain rushed back, and she felt her lip curl a little as she at last saw past his good looks to the person underneath. Just as she'd expected, Lucas Grant was spoiled. And arrogant. And rude.

She ignored the fact that she'd hated having his meal leave her kitchen so unadorned and flavorless—that was beside the point. She was standing right in front of him, and he'd insulted her without a thought.

"Why on earth would you agree to such a moronic contract clause?" Lucas growled, all his attention focused on his call.

She'd heard enough. Back stiff, she grabbed the plate from the table and turned toward the kitchen. If he didn't like his lunch, she would make him something else, because that was what she was being paid to do. But it was going to be a long four weeks catering to the needs of such a jackass, that was for sure.

"Jesus, Derek, it's not like I meant to kick the freakin' thing. I was *drunk*. And if Candy or whatever her name was hadn't left her bloody thong lying around for people to fall over, none of this would have happened."

He was yelling now, his words echoing off the stone floors and high ceiling as Sophie entered the kitchen.

Shaking her head, she dumped the plate on the counter. On-set accident, her ass. He'd obviously injured himself in some stupid episode that involved women's underwear and too much drink. Why was she even remotely surprised? It was exactly the kind of antic that kept his photograph in the gossip magazines on a regular basis. The man was an overgrown frat boy. End of story.

As for her initial reaction to his undeniable physical appeal— Well, she was only human. And now that she'd been reminded of the true man behind the facade, there would be no return of that unexpected, overwhelming rush of lust she'd felt. Uh-uh, no way, no how. It had been a one-off freak occurrence, never to happen again now that she was in full possession of the facts.

She turned from extracting a deli pack of ham from the fridge to find him standing in front of her—towering over her, really, since she was so short and he was so tall—and once again she was awash with the insane urge to press her body against his, to taste his lips, to run her fingers through his hair and wrap them around his—

"Listen, sorry about that," he said, offering her a small, sheepish smile. "What can I say? My leg hurts like hell, I'm hungry enough to eat a small horse and I wasn't expecting a plateful of grass and white sludge."

His apology should have been insulting. He was still running down her cooking, after all. But the truth was that she wouldn't have been too happy about being presented with such a tasteless plateful of bland, either. Plus, he was smiling at her, and it was amazing to discover how many different colors of amber and gold and topaz there were in the irises of his beautiful eyes....

It was happening again! Sophie gave herself a mental slap. She was *not* going to be mesmerized by him. Without a doubt, his appeal allowed him to get away with murder in life, and she was not going to pander to him when he already had most of the western world at his feet.

"I can make you something else," she offered coolly. "An omelet? A club sandwich, or something more substantial, if that's what you want?"

He shrugged in what she figured he thought was a boyishly rueful way. She narrowed her eyes and staunchly resisted the urge to be charmed.

"Apparently my contract states I have to maintain my current weight, and the studio is concerned I'll pork up if I'm forced to sit around on my butt for too long," he said. He eyed the chicken and cottage cheese, then slowly pulled the plate toward himself. "So, I guess this is me for the next four weeks."

Resting his crutches against the island and cocking one hip against it, he grabbed a fork and began to eat. She watched, fascinated despite herself, until she caught sight of his tongue and something warm lurched in the pit of her stomach. Startled, she forced her gaze away.

She wasn't interested in Lucas Grant's tongue—or anyone else's, for that matter.

Don't you ever wonder what it would be like with someone else?

Brandon's words haunted her yet again. Until Lucas had first appeared in her kitchen, she could have honestly answered no to that question. Which was disturbing for a whole bunch of reasons, really.

Determined to resist the lure of his charisma, Sophie returned the ham to the fridge and grabbed the sponge from the kitchen sink. Even though the counters were pristine, she wiped them down, anyway. Anything to distract herself from the disturbing tendency she felt to reach out and touch him, to find out if he really was as hard and hot as he looked.

"There. Done," Lucas said.

She risked a glance in his direction and saw that his plate was bare. And that he'd switched his attention from food to her. There was a certain glint in his eye that hadn't been there before, she noticed. And a certain quirk to one corner of his mouth, as though he was on the verge of smiling but wasn't quite ready to share the joke. Then his gaze dropped below her face and she realized with a hot flush of awareness that he was checking her breasts out. And then—good Lord!—her thighs and ass.

By the time his gaze had returned to lock with hers, he was smiling fully. A big, enchanting, underwear-dissolving smile that had parts of her sitting up and begging for attention in complete violation of her vow to not buy into his whole roguish playboy routine.

"So. There's a long afternoon ahead, Sophie," he said.

Was it just her, or had his voice dropped an octave? She swore she could feel it rumbling along her nerve endings, smoky and seductive and meaningful.

Like a bunny in car headlights, she froze as he moved closer, using the counter to support himself instead of his crutches. By the time she clued in that she'd allowed him to effectively box her in, she was trapped and it was too late.

"So, are you a local? Can you think of anything fun we could do around here to while away the time?" Lucas asked.

Since when had the word fun sounded so...*dirty?* And enticing?

"I—I'm from S-Sydney," she stuttered.

"Well, there's probably plenty we can come up with if we really put our minds to it," he said.

He was standing so close now that she could feel the heat radiating off his body. Her knees were weak, and her breasts felt heavy with need. Between her thighs, a traitorous heat was building.

Man, but he was sexy.

She inhaled deeply, sucking in his woody after-shave and something else that she suspected was simply hot man. For the first time in her life, she was overcome by the carnal desire to touch and be touched by another human being. It didn't matter that he was most likely a jerk of the first order, that he probably didn't have a sensitive or generous bone in his body. She wanted to have sex with him. She wanted to have him inside her, pounding into her, pushing her harder and faster. She wanted to get down and dirty and hot and sweaty with him.

There was so much need swelling inside her, so much crazy desire to be impulsive, to take the risk, to reach out and take what she wanted instead of being cautious and careful and considerate.... She felt dizzy. Out of control.

Scared.

He took another step forward, one hand finding the counter on either side of her so that she was bracketed within his arms. His eyelids had dropped to half mast as he focused on her mouth with intent.

"I've got a couple of really solid ideas if you'd like to try them on for size," he murmured.

He was going to kiss her. He was going to lean down and press his hard body against hers and his tongue was going to be in her mouth and his hands on her skin.

Without even willing it, her palms flattened against his chest. To push him away. She was almost sure that was what she'd planned on doing. But the second she felt the hard curves of his pecs beneath her hands, instead of pushing him away, her hands fisted into the fabric of his T-shirt, and her arms flexed as she prepared to haul him close so she could act on every one of the wild, illicit fantasies dancing across her mind.

He smiled—a complacent, confident, assured smile—and started to lower his head. Inside her, fear warred with animal, instinctive need.

What am I doing?

The thought was like a flare exploding against a dark night sky.

This wasn't the sort of thing she did, the rational part of her mind screamed at her. She was a calm, ordered, careful kind of person. A thinker, a planner. She liked routine—Brandon had said it just last night, in fact. When he broke up with her after fourteen years of monogamy.

She was Sophie Gallagher, chef and, until recently, engaged to be married. She didn't have sex with strange men, even if they were handsome, famous movie stars. Especially if they were handsome, famous movie stars.

Acting on survival instinct, Sophie used every muscle in her body to shove against Lucas's chest as he closed the final inches between them. Despite his size, he rocked back on his heel, his hands slapping onto the counter to regain his balance.

"Whoa!" he said, an annoyed expression replacing his complacent one.

Ducking, she slipped beneath his arm and escaped the corral he'd created with his body.

"Hey, hey, hey," he said, bemused, as she made tracks for the door. "Where are you going?"

"Dinner is at six." She threw the words over her shoulder, relief flooding her. What a close call.

She'd been seconds away from danger. From doing something irrevocable. Something foolish and crazy.

Thank God she'd come to her senses before it was too late.

4

WHAT THE HELL…?

Lucas shoved a hand through his hair and swore under his breath. One minute they'd been go, the next minute she was gone. Frustrated, he stared down at the erection straining the crotch of his jeans. Clearly, there was no chance of getting any relief in that department in the near future, even though she'd been sending out all the right signals—the heated look in her big brown eyes, the telltale pulse flickering at the base of her throat, the rapid rise and fall of her breasts. God, she'd even grabbed him to pull him closer, an aggressive move that had taken him somewhat by surprise. Not that he didn't like aggressive women—his whole sex life was predicated on the existence of women who came looking for what they wanted from him. He just hadn't expected the move from someone who struck him as being more cuddly and cozy than vixen.

Then she'd shoved him away, nearly knocking him onto his butt, and bolted as though the house were on fire.

He shook his head. He couldn't remember the last time a woman had said no to him. Definitely he couldn't remember the last time he'd had to work to get one into bed.

Frankly, it was damn frustrating. He'd been all set to see if her luscious mouth tasted as good as it looked, then she'd slid out from under his arm, leaving him holding his dick, so to speak.

Which was not a recourse he'd had to resort to for a long time, thank you very much. Although if his johnson didn't stand down soon he might have to seriously consider rediscovering the gentle art of self-fulfillment.

Grabbing his crutches, he hopped to the living room and stared blankly at the huge fireplace. Now that Sophie had nixed his chosen form of entertainment for the afternoon, he was back to being at a loose end.

Which reminded him that he'd forgotten to talk to Derek about relocating from this mountain gulag when he'd reamed him out over the diet earlier. Grabbing his phone, he dialed Derek's cell and, surprise surprise, got his manager's voice mail again.

"Get me out of here," he said bluntly before ending the call.

The afternoon stretched endlessly before him. He had some scripts he could read. Derek would be hassling him to commit to his next project soon, anyway. He might as well get on with them sooner rather than later. Except he wasn't really in the mood for plowing through pages of clichéd dialogue and preposterous plot points.

He could e-mail friends. Read a magazine or a book. Sunbathe. Swim.

None of it appealed.

In the normal course of things, he'd go for a run. A long, punishing run. Then he'd call up some buddies, maybe get his Harley out, go for a cruise somewhere, find some margaritas…

None of which was possible with his leg the way it was.

Man, four weeks of this forced inertia was going to kill him. To add a shiny cherry on top of it all, his armpits were starting to ache from the crutches. Last time he'd had crutches he'd grown to hate the damned things, too, he suddenly remembered. He'd been ten and had slipped running down the stairs at the state home where he'd been assigned, and broken his leg. His cast required wrapping in garbage bags every morning so he could shower. He'd gotten a lot of crap from his house mates about the fall, but everyone had wanted to sign his cast. Between them and the kids at school, he'd had over fifty signatures by the time the cast had come off.

Lucas frowned at the memory. He hadn't thought about the old days for a long time. Not exactly the favorite part of his personal history. He pushed the memory away, back into the past where it belonged. "Never look back" was his personal motto, and it had served him well his entire life.

Turning, he headed for the gym. He could get an upper body workout in, at the very least, even if he couldn't do his legs. That ought to keep Derek and the studio happy. And maybe if he exercised hard enough, he could go all-out and eat something that actually tasted like food for dinner.

He made a disbelieving noise in the back of his throat. The way his luck was running, he'd probably get a celery stick and another sloppy spoonful of cottage cheese, served to him by Sophie dressed in a suit of armor.

"I CAN'T BELIEVE it's over so quickly," Becky said.

Sophie leaned against the pillows on her bed and closed her eyes. Her friend's sympathetic voice was exactly what she needed to hear after the turmoil of nearly jumping a certain shallow actor's bones.

What had she been thinking?

What had *he* been thinking?

On second thought, she didn't really need to ponder that one too much. Lucas was used to grabbing what he wanted from life, like a kid given free rein in a candy store. And even though she patently wasn't the kind of woman he was usually photographed with in the gossip mags, she was the only woman he was likely to see for the next few weeks. It didn't take a genius to do the math.

Thank God she hadn't succumbed. Thank God common sense had come to her rescue in the nick of time.

"Soph? Are you still there?" Becky asked.

Sophie dragged her thoughts away from Lucas—again—and concentrated on what her friend was saying. Right, they were talking about Brandon. About the break-up.

"Sorry, I'm still trying to come to terms with it all," Sophie said. Which was exactly why she'd been so vulnerable to Lucas's predatory charm, she decided, conveniently ignoring the fact that she was the one who had touched him first when she pressed her palms against his chest. His firm, strong chest....

"How are you coping?"

I'm experiencing almost irresistible urges to have sex with a virtual stranger.

"I'm not a blubbering mess, if that's what you mean,"

Sophie said. "But I feel so ripped off that Brandon didn't try to talk to me sooner about how he was feeling. It's like he woke up one day and decided he wanted out and that was it."

There was a telling silence on the other end of the phone before Becky made a noncommittal noise. Frowning, Sophie registered for the first time the full meaning of her friend's earlier words—*I can't believe it's over so quickly.*

So quickly. As though Becky had been expecting it to be over, just not so rapidly.

"Becks?" Sophie asked, encouraging her friend to spill what was on her mind. They had always been honest with each other. It was one of the foundation stones of their friendship.

"Well, it's not like you had no warning, Soph," Beck said apologetically. "I mean, Brandon was always going on about traveling to exotic places, like Africa or South America. And when you didn't want to go, he started taking up all those extra activities—learning Italian, rock-climbing, scuba-diving. Classic restless-man stuff, really."

Sophie's first reaction was to bristle at her friend's assessment, but then the *There's Something About Mary* incident popped into her head again. Along with another incident. Four months ago Brandon had driven into the parking lot behind Sorrentino's in a brand-new car. All the staff had poured out the door to admire the shiny paintwork and breathe in the new-car smell—and she'd just stood in shock that he'd made such a major purchase without consulting her. She'd been so embarrassed at the time, however, that she'd played along as though she had known. They'd talked about it afterward, but she hadn't pushed Brandon to find out what was really going on, why he'd made such a challenging, provocative move without discussing it with her first.

Because, again, she hadn't really wanted to know.

"Look, I should have kept my big mouth shut," Becky said. "It's none of my business."

"It's okay. I think—I think maybe you're right," Sophie said slowly. It was hard to say out loud. "I think maybe I knew for a while that he wasn't happy, that he was restless. I didn't do anything about it because I didn't want anything to change."

There was a long silence as they both digested her confession.

"I'm such an idiot, Becky. Did I kill my relationship?" Sophie asked in a small voice.

"Soph, he could have spoken up, too. It takes two to tango. Maybe you were both hanging on because you've been together so long, neither of you could imagine anything else," Becky said. "I can understand how that might happen."

We've been hiding with each other for too long.

Maybe Brandon was right. It was a scary admission to make, but, oddly, it made her feel less conflicted about the way she'd reacted to Lucas. Maybe, if she and Brandon had actually been treading water for a long time…maybe she was more ready to move on than she'd thought. Maybe that was why she was more angry than sad about the way Brandon had broken up with her. And why she'd reacted so powerfully to the sexual appeal of another man. Maybe she really had fallen out of love with Brandon a long time ago.

"Talk to me, Soph," Becky said, concern rich in her voice. "Do you want me to take a few days off work and come stay with you? I'm worried about you being stuck up there in the mountains on your own."

"I'm not alone. Lucas Grant is here with me," Sophie said absently.

"Sorry. What?" Becky said, clearly stunned.

"Lucas Grant. I told you I was working for Lucas Grant, didn't I?"

"Oh my God." There was a clattering sound, then some fumbling, and finally Becky came back on the line. "I literally dropped the phone. And I think I may need to put my head between my legs. Lucas Grant! I can't believe it."

Sophie laughed at her friend's out-of-character reaction. "He's just an ordinary guy," she said.

"No. No way is he ordinary. He is gorgeous. He is hot. He is a walking god. But he is not, nor will he ever be, ordinary," Becky said fervently.

Sophie shook her head at Becky's over-the-top avowal.

"He's a dirty hound dog, is what he is," she heard herself say before she could self-edit. Did she really want to get into a blow-by-blow description of what had nearly happened in the kitchen? "I'd barely known him an hour before he tried to get me into bed," Sophie said.

Apparently she did.

The phone clattered to the floor again. "Let me get this straight. Lucas Grant wants to sleep with you?"

Becky asked incredulously when she came back on the line. *"And you said no?"*

"Correct."

"Sophie, you do realize that he is supposed to be one of the best lovers in Hollywood, right?"

"Sure. Like there's a poll or something. Maybe he has a survey outside his bedroom for women to fill out," Sophie said disparagingly.

Privately, however, a part of herself she didn't even know existed pricked up its ears. *One of the best lovers in Hollywood.* What would a title like that encompass exactly? she wondered. Technique? Enthusiasm? Or was it more about equipment?

"Apparently he's also got the biggest cock," Becky added in reverent tones.

"Pfffttt. It's probably a rumor his PR agent circulates," Sophie said, struggling to hang on to her cool.

The biggest cock? She wasn't exactly experienced in this area, Brandon being her one yardstick, so to speak, but she figured there'd be some pretty hefty contenders in the running. Tommy Lee, for one. And Lucas was bigger than him?

She squirmed, and was instantly glad that her friend couldn't see her. It was bad enough having this conversation in the first place.

"I can't believe we're even discussing this. I just broke up with Brandon *yesterday,*" Sophie said.

There was a short, appalled silence.

"God, Soph, I'm so sorry. I forgot for a second. Lucas Grant does it for me, you know. He's so… Anyway, you don't want to talk about him anymore.

Although—crazy thought here—what a way to get back in the saddle, so to speak."

"Sorry?"

"You know, move on. With Lucas. And his great big—"

"Thanks, I got it. And it's not going to happen," Sophie said drily.

"If you're sure." There was a world of disappointment in her friend's voice.

"I'm sure."

The sound of her friend's other line ringing in the background signaled the end of their call.

"That's a client call I'm expecting," Becky said apologetically. "But I'll call again soon."

Sophie sat for a long time afterward, trying to pretend she wasn't thinking about what her friend had just divulged.

Lucas Grant was a great lover.

A *generously endowed* great lover.

It had been hard enough dealing with her unruly body's reaction to him in the first place, but now every time she looked at him, she'd be thinking about what Becky had told her.

A part of her wished that Becky hadn't said anything all.

But a bigger part of her didn't.

5

LUCAS WOKE WITH HIS HEART pounding and a film of sweat slicking his body. The sheets were wrapped around his bad leg, causing not a small bit of pain as he struggled to free himself.

Sitting upright, he slid to the edge of the bed and braced his elbows on his thighs, letting his head hang. He hadn't had the nightmare for decades. It had haunted him as a kid for three long years until finally he'd trained himself to wake up whenever the nightmare started to take over his dreams. After all these years it still had the power to rev his engine—he felt as though every muscle in his body was braced for fight or flight, pumped full of adrenaline thanks to his subconscious mind's parlor tricks.

Standing, Lucas hopped into the bathroom and leaned against the marble vanity while he sluiced water over his face and shoulders. When he lifted his head from the basin, his reflection showed a flicker of uncertainty in his eyes.

He didn't do uncertainty. Not by a long shot. For years he'd known exactly what he wanted, and gotten it.

At thirty-five, he was a man operating at the peak of

his powers. He'd achieved all his career goals and had more money than he could spend in ten lifetimes. Life was good. Strike that. Life was great. There was absolutely no reason for him to be feeling tense and restless. And certainly no reason for a moldy old nightmare to resurrect itself.

Briefly his thoughts flashed to the biography. Okay, so it wasn't exactly a stretch to connect the recurrence of his nightmare with the appearance of that damned tell-all book.

His expression was grim in the mirror as he allowed himself to think about what was going to happen when the book came out. If it landed on the right desks, he was going to be hounded by every talk-show host to ever draw breath. Kids he'd shared bunks with in state homes over the years would be dug up, his old house mothers and teachers and foster parents would be interviewed. Everything that had previously been only his would be everyone's to know.

The dark years.

The lonely years.

All the stuff he'd never wanted to see the light of day. The stuff he'd gone to great efforts to bury.

Derek, of course, was convinced the book could only do him good.

"People are going to love you for this," he'd said once he finished reading the advance copy he'd brought around that fateful night. "Self-made man, dragging himself up by his bootstraps. The kid who had nothing becomes the man who has everything. Hell, it's a movie in itself."

Derek had gotten a far-off look in his eye at that point, as if he were about to start tapping away on an typewriter that very second, crafting a smarmy biopic to cement Lucas's status as an object of pity.

Lucas had killed that little fantasy before it could take flight, that was for sure, along with all of Derek's other ideas for capitalizing on the biography's release. Lucas's game plan hadn't changed one iota from his initial gut reaction—ignore it, and hope it went away.

His damp skin was chilled now thanks to the air-conditioning, and he reached for the T-shirt he'd taken off when he'd gone to bed. At ten o'clock, no less. Who went to bed at ten, anyway? Five-year-olds? Nuns? He couldn't remember the last time he'd been in bed so early.

Still, it wasn't as if he had anything better to do, since he hadn't seen hide nor hair of Sophie Gallagher since their almost close encounter in the kitchen. He'd gone down at dinnertime to find the table set and his meal—a goddamned salad with steamed salmon and a midget-size portion of fruit salad—laid out in state for him. After eating alone, he'd exhausted the possibilities of television for a few hours, then finally retreated to bed to read some of his scripts.

Now it was three in the morning, and he was awake. And unlikely to be going back to sleep, the way he was feeling right now.

Grabbing his crutches, he tucked them into his armpits and headed for the door. Just for laughs, he took the broad steps down to the ground floor two at a time, then hopped into the living room. The room was dark and filled with shadows, but he'd identified the liquor cabinet earlier and now honed in on it unerringly. After swigging a mouthful each from three bottles, he identified a nice single-malt scotch and poured himself a generous tumblerful. He could have turned on the light and read the labels, but where was the fun in that?

Grabbing the bottle in one hand and the tumbler in the other, he made his way to the long couch in front of the fireplace. Stretching out along its length, he settled into the cushions and savored the burn of good alcohol sliding down his throat.

Technically, he wasn't supposed to drink in combination with the painkillers he was on. He laughed as he poured himself another generous drink. He'd never been good at coloring within the lines.

As he stared out into the dark night, his thoughts gravitated to the absent Sophie again.

What was her story, anyway? It was possible she was married, of course. He'd checked for a wedding ring—none, but that didn't mean she wasn't. He didn't do married. He didn't do anything that smacked of hassle, trouble or strife. Or, more importantly, commitment. So perhaps it was just as well that Sophie had slipped away from him this afternoon, remembering the way her big brown eyes had stared at him as he'd zeroed in for the kill. She wasn't like Candy-Cindy, ready to barter her body in exchange for a brush with fame. He recalled the feeling he'd gotten from Sophie— that sense of warmth and earthiness.

No, it probably was just as well that nothing had actually happened between them.

He laughed soundlessly as he swallowed another mouthful of scotch.

Who was he kidding? If the opportunity presented itself, he'd take advantage. Hell, he might even go so far as to make an opportunity present itself.

Grinning in the dark, he reached for the bottle to top up his drink again.

HE WAS DRUNK. Or at least he had been at some stage during the night. Even standing a few feet away from him at eight o'clock the next morning, Sophie could smell the alcohol coming off his body—his almost-naked body—stretched out along the couch in a boneless sprawl.

Or maybe naked was a subjective assessment. Some people might consider the skin-hugging, black boxer-briefs and chest-moulding T-shirt he was wearing more than ample clothing. Nudists, for example.

From where Sophie was standing, they barely constituted the description clothing. She could see almost the whole length of his strong, muscular legs—his well-shaped calves, his strong thighs, the bruising around his left ankle and knee. She could see a patch of hard belly where his T-shirt had ridden up. She could see the substantial bulge in his boxer-briefs—a feature she eyed with reluctant speculation after Becky's revelations the previous day. She'd never, ever wondered what a man's penis looked like in her entire life before. Yet here she was, measuring him with her eyes, wondering....

He shifted in his sleep, his forehead furrowing briefly, and she took a step back, terrified he was about to wake up and find her panting over him like a desperado.

God, was she really panting?

Yes, she was. To her everlasting confusion.

How could she want to have sex with someone she had absolutely zero respect for? She was no prude, but she definitely believed that sex had to be accompanied by some kind of mutual liking and respect at the very least.

Didn't it?

She studied his face, noting the way his long dark lashes swept his cheeks, the way his mouth was soft and slightly open in sleep. He looked…vulnerable. Surprisingly so. Without the power of his golden eyes to hold the world at bay, he seemed defenseless, an ordinary mortal like the rest of mankind.

Quickly she corrected herself—he was as unlike an ordinary person as it was possible to get. He lived a life of privilege and indulgence, a life so far removed from her own that it might as well exist on another planet. Just because he looked like a lost little boy when he was asleep was neither here nor there.

He shifted again, and Sophie decided it was well past time for her to back away and pretend she'd never seen him passed out here on the couch. Scanning his beautiful body one last time, she lifted one foot, ready to walk away—

"Seen enough?"

She almost dropped the plate of fruit salad and cottage cheese she was carrying as he opened his eyes and smiled slowly up at her. A shiver of awareness raced up her spine.

"Um. I was just wondering if you were cold," she improvised. "I was going to go get you a blanket."

"A blanket? It's November. The middle of summer."

"But this place is air-conditioned," she said feebly.

"Do I look cold?"

She didn't dare scan his body again. She could feel her face burning with embarrassed heat, and she closed her eyes in mortification. There was no excuse for what she'd been doing—ogling. Sizing him up like a choice grade of meat in the butcher shop. Or like a particularly delicious pair of shoes she'd like to try on and walk around in for a while, see how they made her feel....

"Would you like breakfast out here?" she asked without opening her eyes again.

He surprised her by laughing. "Relax, Sophie. I don't bite. Not unless you want me to."

Her eyes popped open of their own accord and he laughed again.

"I wasn't... I mean, I didn't mean to... You were just lying here, and I I..." She could feel her blush growing hotter by the second, if that were even possible. She was practically incandescent with embarrassment.

His smile had faded and he regarded her closely. "You have the most amazingly clear skin," he murmured, eyes narrowing.

Now she should walk away. Definitely. Except she seemed to be stuck here, glued to the floor by the expression on his face and the tension sizzling between them.

"Anyway, this probably makes us even," Lucas said, the intent look vanishing as he settled back and put his arms behind his head, supremely at ease.

"Excuse me?" she asked, trying not to notice the way

his T-shirt had pulled up, exposing even more of his hard belly.

"I have a little confession to make," he said. His eyes were dancing, she saw. She'd known him less than twenty-four hours, but somehow she instinctively knew that that look meant trouble.

"A confession. Right," she said cautiously.

"Yesterday morning when I got here, I noticed there was a telescope out on the balcony of my room. So I had a look through it."

"Yes?"

"You really should make sure the blinds are down before you start walking around after a shower. Just a tip from someone who's had his fair share of candid paparazzi shots over the years."

Sophie stared at him. What was he saying? *Walking around after a shower? Make sure the blinds are down?*

And then she remembered—she'd wandered around the bedroom naked yesterday for a few minutes, finishing the last of her unpacking.

He'd seen her naked?

Lucas Grant?

Through a telescope, no less?

She was so appalled and at the same time suddenly, freakishly hyperaware of him that she didn't know what to say or do.

He'd seen her *naked?*

"So, you see, this morning kind of makes us even Steven," he said, grinning up at her in a way that told her he was perfectly delighted with himself and the world in general.

"You creep," she said before she could remember that he was a movie star and she the hired help. "Do you know how…creepy it is to spy on someone? To invade their privacy like that?"

"Hey—it was an accident. The telescope was pointed at the window already. I just looked through the damned thing. Maybe the guy who was here before me was a creep, but I'm a victim here as much as you," he said.

He was still grinning, clearly not taking any of this seriously. Sophie felt an almost irresistible urge to upend his breakfast on him. Instead she turned on her heel and marched toward the kitchen.

All the while, her brain was working overtime. How much had he seen? Her boobs? Her butt? *Everything?*

"I swear, whoever put that diet menu together has stock in cottage cheese."

Again she jumped. He was right behind her. How had he caught up with her so quickly and silently? On crutches?

"I mean, look at this stuff," he said, propping his crutches against the island bench, much as he had yesterday. "It's not really cheese. Cheese is tasty. Delicious, even. This is more like yogurt gone wrong."

He smiled at her, another one of his look-how-charming-I-am smiles. She put her hands on her hips.

"Being cute is not going to change the fact that you invaded my privacy," she said.

"Was I being cute? Sometimes I don't notice," he said, his grin broadening.

"Sure you don't," she said repressively.

That made him laugh out loud.

"You know, Sophie, despite first impressions, I think you and I are going to get on just fine," he said, grabbing a piece of pineapple with his fingers and popping it into his mouth.

She tried to ignore the way her breasts tingled when he paused to suck the juice from his fingers.

"We'll hardly see each other," she said distractedly, watching as he selected a strawberry.

"Come on now—that's not very friendly. Not when we're the only two people stuck up here." He took a bite out of the end of the strawberry, his teeth very white against its red flesh.

The tingling feeling spread to her thighs. More specifically, to *between* her thighs.

"I'm not here to amuse and entertain you," she said. She didn't dare look down, but she had a strong suspicion that her nipples were trying to poke twin holes through the front of her T-shirt. Trying to be casual about it, she crossed her arms over her chest.

What was with her damn body, anyway? This man had just admitted to blatantly spying on her, and her body wanted to get busy with him? Did it have no taste? No morals? No standards at all?

"You're not married, are you?" he asked.

She blinked in surprise. "No," she said before she could stop herself, then she could have kicked herself when he nodded with satisfaction.

"No boyfriend?"

"You are unbelievable," she said.

"I'm going to take that as a compliment."

"You shouldn't."

"Ouch," he said, grin still firmly in place as he devoured a slice of melon.

"Does it usually work on women, all this stuff? All the teeth and the naughty looks and the walking around half-naked?" she asked, determined to win back some ground.

In reality, she was way out of her league and they both knew it. She'd sat in cinemas where his face had been projected on the screen twenty feet tall. She'd watched him save the planet, get the girl and punish the bad guys so many times that it was impossible for him not to be brushed with magic, no matter how many times she told herself he was essentially an insubstantial cardboard cutout of a man. He was also a very physically attractive man. Fame and good looks—pretty much a lethal combination in the sex appeal stakes.

"You know, Sophie, I don't really know. Usually I don't have to go out of my way, if you get what I mean," he said, looking vaguely thoughtful. "This is kind of a novelty for me."

She knew it was true that women probably threw themselves at him night and day. He probably had to climb over eager bodies every time he left his house. But still, it made her feel a little disappointed in the rest of womankind. He'd been blessed, sure, but did that mean that everything in life had to come easily to him?

Well, one thing was for sure—*she* wasn't going to come easily for him. It was patently obvious that he saw her as a bit of amusing fluff for him to while away the time with. He'd spotted her through the telescope, apparently not been repelled by what was on display, and now he'd decided to cock his little finger at her and allow her the privilege of enjoying The Lucas Grant Experience.

She might be a babe in the woods after fourteen years with one man—and him her first and only lover at that—but she had her pride. Even if Lucas was the best lover in Hollywood with the biggest schlong, he also had the biggest ego and the biggest sense of entitlement. And he was in for a big disappointment where she was concerned. Starting right now.

"Really? Wow. That's interesting. But I wouldn't want you to waste your time, barking up the wrong tree," Sophie said. She was starting to enjoy herself, now that she was getting into the swing of this whole banter thing.

"You have a tree to bark up?" he asked.

She almost laughed, but she managed to control it. He was too damned charming for his own good.

"I'm a lesbian," she said. "I'm not into men."

He laughed outright. "Sweetheart, you are so not a lesbian," he said in a knowing tone.

"Aren't I?" She cocked an eyebrow at him, then held up a hand and ticked off points on her fingers. "Short hair. I never wear makeup. I haven't shaved my legs or under my arms since Bush Senior was in power. And I'm not interested in you."

She grinned at him. To her delight, he was frowning. Clearly she'd given him pause for thought.

"What about before, when you were staring at me? At my—"

"It's been a long time since I've seen one," she said quickly. "I just wanted to know if they were still as repellent as I remember them being. The answer is yes, by the way."

But he was smiling again, a cocky little quirk of his lips.

"You are so not a lesbian," he repeated.

"I don't care if you believe me or not. All I ask is that you respect my orientation," she said, her chin coming up.

Throwing him a cheery smile, she headed for the door. "Lunch is at one. Don't forget to eat your cottage cheese."

6

Lesbian. Yeah, right.

Lucas laughed all the way up the stairs to his bedroom suite.

Of course, there was the outside possibility that she was speaking the truth. But he wasn't buying it, not by a long shot. The way she'd been eyeing him up earlier when he woke screamed that she was aware of him sexually. Just as he was aware of her. And she'd been wearing a tank top yesterday, and he hadn't noticed even a hint of underarm fuzz.

It was a nice smoke screen, however. He was going to enjoy tearing it down immensely.

Man, but she was a foxy little thing. The more time he spent with her, the more appealing he found her. The way she bit her lip when she was trying not to laugh at something he said. The way she put her hands on her hips when she wanted him to know she was truly, truly outraged. That little wiggle in her walk. Not to mention her amazing skin, and perky little butt. And those breasts….

Rueful, he looked down at the tent forming in the front of his underwear. Sexual frustration was another long-forgotten phenomenon for him. He wasn't sure he was enjoying the trip down memory lane, either. But, surprisingly, he *was* enjoying the whole flirtation thing with Sophie. The challenge. The not knowing. Not that he wasn't sure that they'd wind up in bed eventually. It was inevitable, after all. Two grown adults, four weeks, isolation. Some pretty hot chemistry, even if she wasn't his usual type. Really, it was a foregone conclusion.

His erection twitched.

"Yeah, yeah, I hear you, buddy. Sooner rather than later. I got that," he muttered to his impatient nether regions.

The ring of his cell phone cut into his thoughts and he checked the caller ID. Derek.

"Hey," he said, flopping down onto the bed.

"Yo, Lucas. Sorry I didn't get back to you sooner, but I wanted to make sure I had something lined up for you first."

"What?" Lucas said, confused.

"*Get me out of here?* Ring any bells?" Derek said.

Right. That. He'd almost forgotten how bored and restless he'd been when he'd called Derek yesterday.

"Sure," he said. "I was going a little stir crazy."

But he wasn't feeling bored and restless today. Not by a long shot.

"How does this sound—I've booked a charter yacht for you. A big mother of a thing with everything you ever wanted on board and then some. They'll take you up to the Whitsunday Islands off Queensland, you can cruise around, fish, check out the native flora and fauna," Derek said suggestively. "There are plenty of berths on board, too, so you just have to give the word and I'll round up some folks for you to play with."

"Thanks, mate, but you know what? I think I'm going to stick it out up here," Lucas said.

The words were out of his mouth before he'd even consciously thought them. While he wasn't a man given to enormous amounts of introspection, he knew himself passably well. Did he really think getting Sophie Gallagher into bed was going to keep him occupied for four weeks?

"You sure, now? Don't want you going 'round the bend from boredom."

"I'm cool," Lucas said.

Apparently he did.

"Okay. If you're sure. I could drive up on the weekend if you want some company…?" Derek said.

For some reason the thought of introducing Derek to Sophie made an alarm bell sound deep in the back of Lucas's mind. The thought of her in the same room with his shark-in-a-suit manager didn't feel right. Besides, he didn't want anything breaking the bubble of their isolation. Two's company, three's a crowd, et cetera.

"Nah. I'm kind of enjoying the peace and quiet. I'll see you in four weeks' time," Lucas said.

Ending the call, Lucas stared at the ceiling for a beat. The truth was, he realized with surprise, he genuinely *was* starting to enjoy the peace and quiet a little.

Go figure.

Shucking his clothes and hopping to the shower, Lucas turned his mind back to the conunundrum that was Sophie. Yesterday he'd pursued her casually, almost as an afterthought. This morning his interest had become a whole lot more personal. She'd become a challenge. And he was looking forward to conquering her.

Which meant it was time to step things up a notch. Accordingly, when he finished showering he used some of his signature aftershave, a scent created especially for him by Kenzo. His stubble was one day old and needed no help from him to look suitably bad-boy disreputable—something he knew from vast experience was catnip for the female of the species.

Standing in front of his suitcase—he still hadn't gotten around to unpacking—he pursed his lips, thinking through the clothing options. Then he grinned as inspiration struck and he grabbed his board shorts. The pool. What better place to take things up a notch? Technically he was supposed to spend as much time as possible wearing his ankle and knee braces, but what his doctors didn't know wouldn't hurt them.

Five minutes later Lucas's crutches ate up the pathway leading to the caretaker's lodge. The morning sun was warm on his bare chest as he knocked on Sophie's door. Typical of an Australian summer, it was going to be a stinker of a day.

She made him wait a long time before he heard footsteps approaching. He smiled as he imagined her going over her options: ignore him and pretend she wasn't home—almost impossible to pull off given the circumstances—or suck it up and deal with him again.

She had her game face on, he saw, when she opened the door, but he had the satisfaction of seeing her eyes round when she took in his bare chest.

"Thought we could go for a swim," he said.

"Did you?" She was working really hard to keep her gaze above his chin. He leaned forward so she could get a noseful of his aftershave.

"Yeah, I did. The water's great, the sun's out. Have you got anything better to do?"

She opened her mouth to protest, but he reached out and pressed a finger against her lips. They were incredibly soft, and he added them to the increasingly long list of things that were beginning to fascinate him about her.

"Before you say it, I get it. You're not into guys. I respect that. But it doesn't mean we can't hang out while we're up here, right? I swear I'm going to go a little nuts if we don't," he said.

She hesitated a moment, then shrugged. "Okay," she said cautiously. "I'll meet you by the pool."

"I'll wait," he said, propping his hip against the door-frame. He wasn't about to give her time alone to second-guess herself. He'd only known her a short while, but he got the feeling she was the kind of person who would think things to death if given half the chance.

She opened her mouth to protest, then closed it again without saying a word. Frowning, she turned on her heel and headed down the hall. He would bet she came out fully clothed, her swimsuit carefully concealed.

Because she'd left the door open, he leaned forward and stuck his nose inside, taking quick stock of her accommodation. Polished floors led the way into a small galley-style kitchen, and beyond that he could see a living room. No doubt her bedroom was off that somewhere. It wasn't as ostentatiously high-end as the main house, but it was warm and inviting and full of light.

He heard a door open and promptly retreated to his original waiting place outside the door. She appeared, carrying a towel and wearing a T-shirt and shorts. The only telltale sign that she intended to swim was the bright aqua tie visible around her neck. He'd nailed it in one. He was also pretty sure that she was wearing a sedate one-piece under all that clothing, too. She just wasn't the bikini kind of woman. Not that he cared too much. There was only so much modesty a bathing suit could afford, after all.

"Water's warm," he said by way of encouragement as she walked silently before him in the direction of the pool.

But he was the one who lost the power of speech when she stopped by the closest lounger and stripped off her T-shirt. Full breasts spilled out of two scraps of aqua Lycra.

Thank you, God. She was wearing a bikini, after all. Showed how much he knew.

As he stared unrepentantly, she stuck her thumbs into the waistband of her shorts and tugged them down, revealing a pair of snug boy-cut hipster bottoms. When she turned toward the pool, he leered with outright hunger at her great, round little butt.

Oh yeah. Going for a swim had been an excellent idea, if he did say so himself.

Now all he had to do was to get her wet and willing.

"Last one in is a rotten egg," he said, throwing his crutches to one side and leaping into the water.

SOPHIE HESITATED on the edge of the pool. He surfaced, his hair slicked to his skull, his skin gleaming with water.

How could he look even better wet than he did dry? It truly was unfair.

Not that it mattered one way or the other to her now that she was a committed lesbian.

"Don't make me come and get you," he called, sending a warning splash her way.

"What about your injury?" she asked. "Don't you have some kind of brace thing you're supposed to be wearing?"

He made a dismissive noise. "It'll be fine. Come on, get your ass in here."

For some reason the way he said ass made her feel acutely self-conscious. It also reminded her that he'd seen her naked.

Why couldn't she get that fact out of her mind? And it wasn't because she was outraged that he'd invaded her privacy, or whatever other drivel she'd thrown at him in the kitchen. Rolling her eyes, she forced herself to acknowledge the truth: she hated the thought that he might compare her to other women he'd slept with and find her wanting.

She knew for a fact that he'd starred in movies with Cameron Diaz, Halle Berry and Jessica Alba. And that he'd been paired with supermodels like Naomi Campbell and Tyra Banks in the gossip pages. Not a group of women she wanted to compete with on any level, except perhaps in the kitchen.

Not that she *was* competing, because she was a lesbian now.

God, she was so screwed up. And it was all his fault. His and Brandon's. Because if Brandon hadn't wanted out of their comfortable rut, if he hadn't poked her with a stick and pointed out that life was elsewhere, she wouldn't be in this stupid situation in the first place.

Pinching her nostrils with one hand, she launched herself into the air, tucking one knee tight to her chest and dropping into the water with a highly satisfactory splash. With a bit of luck, Mr. Cocky had just scored a load of backwash in his face.

She sank to the bottom of the pool, bubbles fizzing off her skin as she bent her knees to absorb the gentle impact, then used her thigh muscles to bounce back toward the surface.

He let her get a single mouthful of air before splashing her in the face.

"Nice bomb," he said. "You have brothers, right?"

"Nope."

"Sisters, then? Tough, lesbian sisters just like you?"

She hesitated. It was always difficult answering this question. If she said no, she felt like she was denying Carrie ever existed. If she said yes, she opened up a can of worms....

"I had a sister. She died in a car accident when I was fifteen," she said matter-of-factly.

"I'm sorry," he said after a short silence.

She shrugged. "It's a long time ago, now."

He looked uncomfortable, and she took pity on him.

"What about you? Any brothers or sisters?" she asked.

"Nope. Only child."

He splashed her in the face again, and she spluttered as water went up her nose.

"Nice," she said. "Hope you've got eyes in the back

of your head, because you're going to need them. I'm one of those feisty redheads who believes in payback."

"Is that a threat?" he asked.

"I'd like to think it's more of a promise," she said.

He laughed and took off down the pool with a powerful freestyle, using only his arms to propel him through the water. She followed at a more leisurely pace, doing a number of slow laps before finally coming to a halt in the shallow end of the pool.

"I think that's it for me," she said. "I'm turning into a prune."

He raised his eyebrows at her. "What about your revenge?"

She waved a hand negligently in the air. "That old thing? Pfff."

Turning her back on him, she climbed the steps out of the pool. She waited until he'd resumed his laps before finding a spot along the edge, lining him up, and waiting for him to come within range. With a banshee cry, she leaped into the air and bombed him again, sending a very impressive shot of water straight up his nose, if she didn't miss her guess. Giggling like an idiot, she struck out for the steps and was out of the pool before he could even lunge after her.

He stood in the shallow end, water sluicing off his body as he pushed his hair off his forehead.

"Okay, I'll pay that one," he said, nodding in grudging admiration. "If I didn't have this leg…"

"Sure, sure. Whatever," she said, suddenly terribly aware of exactly how much excitement was bubbling through her blood, and how much she was enjoying his company, and how very, very delicious he looked, all wet and golden and almost naked. Without her permission, her eyes mapped the planes of his chest and belly, lingering on the trail of dark hair that disappeared beneath the low-slung waistband of his board shorts.

Lesbian, she reminded herself. *You're into women, not men. Definitely not hairy men, with big, muscly shoulders and arms and chests and six-pack abs and whatever else is hiding beneath all that wet fabric.*

He was laughing at her, his hands planted on his hips, and she knew the exact moment that she'd stared at him too long—he got that predatory gleam in his eye again. For someone who didn't usually have to do anything to attract women, he seemed to be taking an awful lot of pleasure in hunting her down.

She only hoped he knew how to handle failure.

"I might get a bit of sun now," she said, turning away from his knowing look.

"Great idea," he said.

Crossing to her lounger, she spread her towel out and lay down on her belly. The sun was warm on her skin, and she guessed she'd be dry within a matter of minutes.

"You'll burn," he said from close by, and she realized that he'd settled in the lounger next to hers.

Surprise, surprise.

"I've got some lotion," he said, and before she could explain that she'd planned on simply drying off for a few minutes in the sun before seeking the shade, she felt a large blob of something warm and gooey land in the middle of her back.

She raised herself up onto her elbows and found

Lucas sitting on her lounger now, looking as if he was settling in for the duration.

"What are you doing?" she asked with exaggerated patience.

"Saving you from yourself. This skin of yours will go up like a torch," he said.

They both knew that it was an excuse for him to touch her. For a moment she stared at him, more words of protest on the tip of her tongue. Then he started to rub the cream in, his fingers firm, his strokes wide and sweeping, his eyes daring her to call him on what he was doing, and she decided discretion was the better part of valor.

That, and it felt pretty good, too.

Okay, that was an understatement. Because he wasn't just rubbing the lotion in, he was massaging it in, his fingers digging into her muscles, his palms pressing down firmly. It was fantastic. Delicious. Addictive. Flopping back down, she gave herself up to the experience. She'd already prepared his salad for lunch and left it in the fridge in the main house. Workwise, she was footloose and fancy free till later in the day. Sighing, she gave herself up to indulgence.

"This thing's in the way," he murmured after a few minutes, and she felt a tug on the back of her bikini top as he undid both the top and bottom ties.

Vaguely she knew she should say something. Something about him not undoing what little clothing she was wearing. What self-respecting lesbian allowed a man to undress her, for Pete's sake? But it felt so good, and she hadn't realized how much tension she'd been carrying in her shoulders over the past few days….

Just a few minutes, she promised herself. *Just a few stolen, decadent minutes.*

"So, how long have you been gay? If that's not too personal a question," Lucas asked as she was about to dissolve into a boneless, gooey puddle and slide right off the lounger.

"Sorry? Um. Since my early twenties," Sophie said, forcing her sluggish brain into action.

"Hmm. So you must have a lot of experience with the, uh, ladies," he said.

There was a trap coming, and she knew it, but she also didn't know how to avoid it.

"Sure. Yeah, I guess you could say that," she said, trying to sound worldly.

"Great. I've always wanted to get a few tips from an expert," Lucas said.

A spurt of alarm—and something a lot hotter and more liquid—shot through her as she felt him fold down the waistband of her bikini bottoms and start rubbing lotion into the small of her back and the top of her butt.

"Um. Okay," she said, knowing she should stop his roving hands but loving what he was doing to her.

"Mostly I'm interested in oral sex," he said.

"Oral sex?" she repeated, biting her lip as he found a particularly tender spot in the small of her back and attacked it with his thumb.

"Mmm. So, what's your best advice on technique? Generally speaking, in my experience, it seems to me that it's all about good tongue work."

Sophie froze. Were they really having this conversation? Was she really going to lie here, with his hands on her skin, and discuss oral sex?

"I like to start out gently, a bit of kissing, maybe some nibbling," he said, his thumbs massaging the muscles either side of her spine now. "Then I like to work my way in, build things up a bit. Use my hands as well as my mouth."

She swallowed. Even though she knew exactly what he was doing, she could still feel damp heat building between her thighs. Just the thought of him between her legs, his dark hair a stark contrast to her pale skin, his mouth open on her, his tongue tasting her, teasing her… She pressed her face harder into the towel and fought the urge to wriggle her hips.

She should tell him to stop. Right now. She should call a halt to this…whatever it was.

His hands had dropped to her sides now, his fingers lightly teasing their way down to where the swell of her breasts spilled out on either side of her body. His fingers danced across her skin, hot and knowing, and her breasts grew heavy with desire. Between her legs, desire throbbed. She was so turned on, she felt as though she was about to melt from the inside out.

"After building things up, I like to move in for the kill. Find her sweet spot, and just go to town," he said, his voice barely a murmur now. "Fast, then slow, sucking, licking, teasing. Sometimes, I—"

It was too much. She couldn't take another second of it. The sensuous torture of his hands on her body, the erotic promise of his words—something had to give.

Acting on impulse, she shoved herself up on her elbows and twisted around to face him.

"All right, okay. I'm not gay. You got me. Happy?" she told him.

Too late she remembered that he'd undone her bikini top. She felt his hot gaze on her bare breasts, could almost feel his touch on her already-hard nipples, and muscles she didn't even know she had tightened in anticipation inside her.

"Never, ever feel bad about not being a lesbian," Lucas said.

And then he leaned forward and kissed her.

She wasn't sure what happened next. His lips on hers, his tongue in her mouth, his hands closing around her aching breasts—it all seemed to blur into one big explosion of sensation. Before she knew it she was being pulled into his lap—or did she crawl there?—and her legs were straddling his waist, and her skin was against his, and a ferocious tide of need was building inside her.

He felt so good. He was so hard, his tongue so wet and knowing in her mouth. She slid her fingers into his hair, fisting her hands in case he tried to break their kiss before she'd drunk her fill of him.

She needed… She wanted…*everything*.

He was playing with her breasts, squeezing her nipples gently, then soothing them with his palms, and she sobbed in the back of her throat and tilted her hips, all mindless instinct and greedy demand.

He murmured his approval, one hand leaving her breasts to sweep down her belly and slide beneath the waistband of her bikini bottoms. She was wide open to him sitting the way she was, and he slid his fingers through her curls and straight onto her clitoris. She earned another murmur of approval as he felt how wet and ready she was for him. He pressed gently down on her swollen clit with one finger, sending a shock wave racing through her body.

She broke their kiss, suddenly overwhelmed by the urges gripping her. She wanted to rip off his clothes and get him inside her. She wanted to ride him hard, scratch his back, lick him, bite him. She wanted to be utterly filled by him, stretched, owned.

It was too much. It was too scary, too uncontrollable. She'd never felt this way before. Never. And she didn't know how to contain it, how to control it, how to keep it safe.

"I can't do this," she said abruptly, her whole body shaking as she wrenched herself away from him.

Arms crossed over her chest, Sophie turned tail and bolted for the caretaker's cottage.

7

HER PHONE WAS RINGING when she stumbled into the cottage. She glanced at the caller ID, ready to ignore it since she appeared to be smack-dab in the middle of a nervous breakdown, then paused when she saw it was her mother.

She'd left a message for her parents that morning, before she'd gone out to the pool. She'd wanted to tell them what had happened before they called the apartment and heard it from Brandon.

Now her finger hovered uncertainly over the talk button, but suddenly the sound of her mother's voice seemed like a very needful thing. She pressed the button.

"Mom, hi," she said, moving into the bedroom to pull on a T-shirt. Her body was still humming with desire and confusion, and she almost sighed with relief when she heard her mother's familiar tones.

"Sophie. I'm sorry we missed you this morning, sweetheart. How are things?" Laura Gallagher asked.

"Okay." Sophie tried to gather her thoughts. Not easy, given what she'd just run away from. God, she was such an idiot.

"Look, Mom, there's no easy way to say this, so I'm just going to say it. Brandon and I have broken up. It was mutual, mostly. And we're both okay. I've taken four weeks off from work to do a private catering job, but I'll probably look for a new job and a new apartment when I get back to Sydney," Sophie said in a rush.

There was a long silence before her mother spoke again. "Well, I can't say I'm surprised."

Sophie sank onto the end of the bed. "Really?"

"Sweetheart, neither of you have been very happy for a long time now. Everyone could see that," her mom said.

Everyone, apparently, except for Sophie. She felt a prickle of irritation. "I suppose you're going to tell me that Brandon and I have only been staying together because we were too scared to move on, as well," she said a little sharply.

"Did someone else say that to you?"

"Brandon. And Becky, in a roundabout way."

"I see."

"Great. So you think I'm a coward, too." In the back of her mind, she knew she was overreacting, lashing out at her mom because she was so confused over what had happened with Lucas. Because she'd run away from him, hadn't she?

So maybe she *was* a coward.

"I don't think you're a coward, sweetheart. In some ways I think you're one of the strongest people I know," her mother said.

For some reason, tears sprang to Sophie's eyes. God, she was so messed up.

"Okay," she said, sniffing her tears back.

"Maybe you can't see it right now, but I think this will be a good thing for you, Soph. I've often wondered if you and Brandon would have lasted as long as you did had you not gotten together around the time that Carrie died."

Sophie frowned. "What's that got to do with anything?" she asked.

"You were very upset afterward. And Brandon was the boy next door. And he was so kind and reliable and patient. I understood what drew you to him."

"You make him sound like a security blanket, not a boyfriend," Sophie said.

Wisely, her mother chose to change to the subject.

"I was thinking about you and your sister the other day. Your father got all our old home movies put onto DVD, and we were watching some of them. You two were such tearaways. I'd forgotten how much trouble you used to get into together."

Sophie shuffled farther back on the bed and tucked her knees into her chest. There had only been eighteen months between her and Carrie, and they'd been each other's best friends. Carrie had always been so colorful and bold and adventurous. Sophie had adored her. She knew her parents had been worried out of their minds by some of her sister's antics, especially when she grew older and discovered boys—and they discovered her.

"That time you two went into the city and came back with all that racy lingerie! My God, I wanted to die when I realized you must have stolen it all. I was going to make you take it back to each store and apologize in person, you know. But then Carrie took the car out that night…." Her mom trailed off into sad silence. They both knew how the story ended, how Carrie had rolled the car secretly down the driveway, started it in the street and gone joyriding with her boyfriend, Jake. How they'd misjudged a curve in the road and plowed straight into a big old gum tree.

But Sophie was frowning over something else her mother had said.

"I didn't shoplift with Carrie," she said. "Are you kidding? I'm way too scared of getting caught to try to pull something like that off."

"Sophie," her mother said gently, "you were both giggling like maniacs when I found you in your room. And half the stuff was your size. You even bragged to me about how quick you were and how no one would ever catch you."

Sophie shook her head. "No. I would remember that. I know I would," she said.

"Well, you were very upset after she died. And I know it was hard on you, since you'd shared a room all your lives. That's why your father and I wanted to take the second bed out of your room after a few months. But you wouldn't let us."

"It was hers," Sophie said.

"I'll be honest, there was a part of me that was grateful that you calmed down so much afterward. You took up with Brandon, and you applied yourself at school more. But I used to worry that maybe a part of you died with Carrie, too."

"I can't remember any of this. All I can remember is how amazing she was. Larger than life."

"You both were. Remember the time when Mrs. Hartley from next door caught you sneaking out your bedroom window to go to the movies? She marched you 'round to the front door and gave you a lecture in front of us. The next day we woke up and every single flower on her prize rosebush had been deadheaded. I never did get you to admit to it."

Sophie pulled her knees closer to her chest. Now that her mother had prompted her, she could remember the incident. Remember, too, conspiring in the dark with Carrie to carry out Operation Payback in the early hours of the morning. Since she was already in trouble, Sophie had insisted that Carrie stay in bed so she could honestly say she had nothing to do with it if their parents asked.

"I'm sorry. I'm upsetting you. I didn't mean to," her mom said after Sophie hadn't spoken for a while.

"I'm not upset," Sophie said. Then she felt something hot and wet drip onto her knee and realized she was crying. Swallowing a lump of emotion, she fought for control.

"You know what? You should come up and stay with us for the weekend," her mom said.

"I can't, Mom. This job I have is seven days a week."

"Good heavens. Sounds like slave labor."

Sophie considered what she'd almost done with Lucas out by the pool. Nope. Definitely not slave labor.

"It's actually pretty easygoing," she said.

They talked for a few minutes more before ending the call. Sophie sat for a long time afterward, thinking over what her mother had said.

Once upon a time, she'd been larger than life, just like her crazy, impulsive, magical sister. Why had she chosen to forget that part of herself? It was almost as though after Carrie died, she'd reinvented herself into some perfect little Stepford Sophie.

Why?

With a flash of intuition, Sophie remembered how she'd felt when she'd been in Lucas's arms earlier. Out of control. And scared. Absolutely terrified—if she were being completely honest with herself—of what might happen if she let herself go, if she gave free rein to the wildness inside her.

Was that what she'd learned from her sister's death? To be scared? That impulsiveness and craziness and wildness were dangerous, dangerous urges to give in to?

Pressing her face against her bare knees, Sophie sobbed hot tears as she allowed herself for the first time in years and years to remember the loneliness of their shared bedroom after her sister's death. The empty bed. The empty half of the closet. The horrible guilt that she'd known about her sister's plans to sneak the car out, had even watched TV with her parents in case a distraction was needed.

"I'm sorry," she mumbled into her knees. "I'm so sorry I never stopped you."

She didn't try to stop the tears, because she knew they had to come—guilty, scared tears that had been locked inside her for fifteen years. Then, when the storm had passed, she took a long shower and made herself hot tea and toast and sat on the window seat in the living room and stared out at the world as the day faded to dusk.

Finally she stood, her moves decisive, her step firm

as she walked to the bathroom to assess her face. Her eyes were a little pink, but she figured that only a close friend would guess that she'd been crying.

Good. Because there was something she needed to do.

Something for herself.

Something brave and bold and a little wild.

No matter how much it scared her.

No matter how strong the urge was to stay in control.

The sliding door from the terrace slammed back on its well-oiled track as she shoved it open and entered the main house. She strode into the living room, a woman on a mission.

"Lucas?" she called, her voice echoing in the empty space.

Silence. He must be upstairs.

She bounded up the deep, shallow steps, determination driving her on.

"Lucas?"

She found him on the bed in the master suite, lying with his arms crossed behind his head, glaring at the ceiling as though it had done him wrong in some way.

"Listen—" he said when he saw her, but she cut him off.

"Is your offer still good? The one you made earlier by the pool?"

He looked confused.

"Do you still want me?" she clarified boldly.

He frowned. "Yes, but—" She cut him off again with the simple expedient of jumping on the bed and straddling his body.

"Shut up and kiss me," she demanded.

Lucas didn't need to be asked twice.

Reaching up, he slid his hands into Sophie's hair as she pressed her body against his and kissed him, her tongue sliding inside his mouth to taste him with teasing, darting strokes. Her thighs straddled his hips and her breasts pressed into his chest, and he wanted her naked so bad that he ached with it. He was as hard as a rock, and he slid his hands down to her waist and ground himself into her. Probably a civilized man would ask questions about why she'd freaked out earlier, but right now he was pure caveman. And the only thing that mattered was that he wanted her, and she wanted him.

Intent on satisfying their mutual desire, he glided his hands up Sophie's torso and under her T-shirt and discovered she wasn't wearing a bra. Smart lady.

She groaned her approval as he cupped her breasts, breaking their kiss to sit up and take over the task of undressing herself, whipping her T-shirt over her head. Her full breasts bounced as she rolled to one side, pushing her shorts down to reveal a neat, silky thatch of curls that drew his gaze like a magnet. He'd been so busy enjoying the view and her enthusiasm for getting naked that he'd forgotten his own clothes, but he suddenly realized that one of them was grossly overdressed. She helped him drag his workout shorts down his legs and over his knee and ankle brace in one hit.

"Help me with these stupid things," he said, and for a brief moment there was only the sound of tearing Velcro as she helped him free his bad leg.

Then they were both naked, and there was nothing standing in the way of the hard, throbbing need between his legs connecting with the wet, hot spot between hers. Grabbing a condom from his bedside drawer, he took care of protection in record time.

"Come here," he instructed, hauling her on top of him, and they both gave a sigh of relief as bare skin met bare skin.

"You feel so good," he murmured into her neck as he kissed her there, his hands gliding up and down her soft, silky body. The curve of her hip, the roundness of her ass, the dip of her waist—he discovered them all with his hands before taking possession of her breasts. She was everything he'd anticipated and more. Sexy. Vibrant. Hungry.

She gasped her approval as he toyed with her breasts, her hips circling as she rubbed her wet center against his straining erection.

More than anything he wanted to bury himself inside her and go for broke, but she was so amazingly responsive, so vocal, so lost in the moment that he wanted to give her as much pleasure as possible before taking her. Her eyes were tightly shut, and the naked desire on her face was an incredible turn-on. Hauling her body up his chest, he pulled a nipple into his mouth and sucked hard, flicking his tongue rhythmically over and over the tight peak. She shuddered, her fingers digging into his shoulders, her hips circling once more as she blindly sought satisfaction. Determined to give her everything she needed, he slid a hand down her belly and into the curls between her thighs. She was so hot and wet and ready for him he almost lost it, and when he delved into her delicate folds, her thighs tightened around his hips and her fingers clenched even harder on his shoulders.

He found her clit for the second time that day, swollen and ready for him, and he teased it with his fingers, circling, rubbing, flicking. She moaned, pushing herself down onto his hand, and when he finally slid a finger inside her she hissed a four-letter word and began to ride his hand as though there was no tomorrow.

He couldn't stand it. She was the hottest thing he'd ever had in his bed—absolutely abandoned, nothing but raw instinct, unashamed to take what she wanted. He couldn't wait a moment longer, and he withdrew his hand from her and reached for her hips in one move.

She barely had time to register a protest before he'd positioned himself at her entrance.

"Yes," she encouraged in an earthy husk, grabbing his shaft with a greedy hand and holding him steady as she rubbed her slick folds against the head of his erection. He closed his eyes and gripped her hips and thrust mindlessly into her, and she let him slide inside in one silken stroke. She was so hot, so tight, so right. He clenched his teeth and hung on to sanity by a thin, thin thread.

"Yessss," she sighed, and he opened his eyes again to take in the sight of her as she rode him, thighs spread wide, head thrown back, breasts thrust out, mouth open as she panted her need.

Capturing her breasts in his hands, he thrust up into her as she circled her hips. A delicate flush covered her chest, and he felt her thighs clench against him as she neared her climax. Once again he sent a hand delving where their two bodies became one, wanting to see her fall apart, wanting to push her over the edge. Her eyes opened as he found her and slicked his thumb firmly back and forth, her breasts rising as she sucked in one last, final breath before her orgasm took her. He felt the pulsing of her inner muscles around his shaft, and finally he let himself go, grasping her hips in both hands as he pumped up into her, grinding his hips into hers, the muscles of his arms and neck corded as he rode toward his own climax.

And then he lost it, his head pressing back into the bed as he shuddered out his release into her hot, tight little body, his breath rasping harshly in his throat as he came and came and came.

Afterward, he lay boneless and exhausted, staring blankly up at the ceiling. That had been…incredible. The hottest encounter of his life, hands down. Just thinking about it, about her, made him want to go all over again. She was panting beside him on the bed, and he turned his head to look at her. Her breasts rose and fell, rose and fell, and his cock throbbed. She'd been so tight, so hot. And the way she'd given herself up to the moment, the rush…

She rolled onto her side, propping her head up with one arm. Her cheeks were flushed, her nipples still hard with arousal. Man, he wanted another taste of her.

"I'm not sure what the etiquette in these situations is, but thanks," she said. "That was amazing."

He was about to reply when she reached out and ran a hand across his chest, a look of intense concentration on her face.

"You have such an amazing body. And your cock… When you slid inside me it was the most incredible feeling—" She broke off with an embarrassed laugh. "Sorry. I'm probably not supposed to say that, either, am I?"

"Trust me, no man is going to knock back a compliment like that," he said.

"I was a little nervous about what it would be like with another man, to be honest. Huh." She shook her head, amused by her own thoughts.

An alarm bell went off in the back of his mind. Hadn't she said she wasn't married? So what was all this talk about another guy?

"You didn't just make an adulterer out of me, did you, Sophie?" he asked, keeping his tone light.

"What? No! No way. I told you I'm not married. I just… I'm just recently single, that's all." The words sounded awkward, as though she wasn't used to saying them yet.

He frowned, a suspicion forming.

"How recent?"

She shrugged a shoulder, making her breasts jiggle deliciously. He was so busy admiring them that he almost missed her reply.

"Sunday."

"This Sunday? The one just passed? Two days ago?"

She nodded. "Fourteen years. But it was time to move on." She looked embarrassed for a moment, as though she was considering not saying what was on her mind. Then she spoke again. "We'd been together since high school. He was the only other guy I'd ever…you know, been with. Apart from you, of course. So now I have two notches on my belt."

She laughed self-consciously, and if he hadn't been preoccupied with freaking out, he would have admired how pretty and sexy and appealing she looked with a little post-sex color in her cheeks.

He closed his eyes as the extent of what he'd just done hit him: he'd slept with a virtual virgin. Belatedly he remembered the way she'd bolted from the pool earlier. At the time, he'd decided that she was more trouble than she was worth, no matter how fascinated he'd become with her. Then she'd turned up unexpectedly in his doorway and his dick had taken charge of any and all decision-making.

And the really, really great thing was, he was stuck up here with her for four weeks. He almost groaned as he imagined the kind of complications he'd invited into his life. She'd expect things—of course, she'd expect things. Something he probably should have thought about before he had taken a trip to Blissville inside her.

He opened his eyes and glanced at her again. She'd flopped onto her back and was staring into space, a small smile curving her lips.

Man, he was such an idiot. She was probably picking out china patterns, or—at the very least—imagining that they were now involved in some kind of meaningful relationship.

He was opening his mouth to dispel her of any and all illusions when she sat up.

"I'm going to have a shower. Do you mind?"

"Go for it," he said.

Even in the midst of bachelor-panic he could admire

her tidy little body—those great breasts, that sweet double handful of an ass.

She paused on the threshold of the bathroom and looked back at him over her shoulder.

"If you wanted to, you could, um, join me," she said.

Like one of Pavlov's dogs, his cock sprung to life.

Pathetic.

But what the hell? One more round of madness, then he'd make sure they were both on the same page.

Following her into the bathroom, he hopped into the double shower cubicle with her. She eyed his hard-on avidly. Without saying a word, she reached for the soap and began to rub it over his body, starting with his chest, moving slowly on to his belly, one hand wielding the soap, the other following afterward, working in slow, sensuous circles across his skin.

All the while, she studied his body, her lips slightly parted, her expression intent.

"Turn around," she ordered, and he braced himself against the corner as she worked her way down his back, her small hands firm and thorough. When she came to his butt, she put the soap down and moved up behind him, cupping his cheeks in both hands.

"I've wanted to do that from the moment I first saw you," she said quietly. She squeezed him gently, learning the shape of him, her breasts pressed against his back the entire time.

He closed his eyes, enjoying the slow build. Finally, she slid her soap-slicked hands around his waist and reached for his hard-on, working his shaft, sliding right up to his head, her strokes firm and knowing.

After a few minutes she stepped away from him. "Turn around again."

Once again her gaze ate him up hungrily—his shoulders, his chest, his stomach, his cock. He couldn't remember another woman ever taking the time to know him so well, to really look at him, to savor the act of touching so fully.

One hand on his chest, she slowly sank to her knees, the hot water pounding down on both of them. Then she was taking him in her mouth, one hand grasping his shaft, the other sliding around his waist to grab his butt and pull him closer.

As if he wanted to be anywhere else.

She licked, she sucked, she teased. Her tongue laved the head of his cock, sometimes hard and firm, sometimes fast and fleeting. She built him slowly, steadily, and then she took him over the edge.

Afterward, she rose to her feet, licking her lips.

"You do taste as good as you look," she said. Then she laughed. "God, I can't believe I just said that."

Which made her laugh again. He found himself grinning, too, and pulling her close for a kiss. She pressed herself against him and opened her mouth to him.

Picking up the soap, he washed her in the same attentive, thoughtful, sensuous way that she'd washed him. Her small, square shoulders. Her full, incredibly responsive breasts. Under her arms—where there was not a sign of hair, he noted. Smiling as he remembered the lesbian gambit, he washed her belly, enjoying the softness of her, and the encouraging sounds she made as he soothed her skin in the wake of the soap. Cupping her butt in one hand, he slid the bar of soap between her legs and slicked it across her folds, back and forth, back and forth. She closed her eyes and began to pant.

Ridiculous to be jealous of a bar of soap—especially one he was wielding—but he was. Letting it fall from his hand, he slid his fingers between her legs instead. She braced an arm against the shower wall and leaned her forehead against his chest, moaning softly as he worked her.

She was incredible. Utterly in the moment. A slave to sensation.

Then she was pushing against his fingers and her whole body was trembling as she approached her climax. Her free hand found his shoulder and slipped around his neck and she pressed her face into his chest, gasping out her pleasure.

He waited until her body softened before withdrawing his hand. At about the same time, he noticed that his cock had recovered. Not a record, but close. Because she was so hot, and he was so hot for her.

"Let's go find some dry land," he murmured against her neck.

She laughed and reached out to turn the shower off. As he helped her dry off, he remembered that little talk he'd been meaning to have.

It could wait for the morning. After all, there were so many games they had left to play in that king-size bed.

SOPHIE WOKE feeling utterly rested, and ever so slightly stiff. Last night—and early this morning—she'd used muscles she didn't even know she had.

She smiled to herself as she remembered the shower. Then, afterward, the bed. Another two times. He was insatiable. She was insatiable. They'd finally fallen asleep out of sheer exhaustion.

She bit her lip on a ridiculous, inappropriate laugh as she remembered Becky's claim that Lucas was reputed to be one of the best lovers in Hollywood. *Try the world,* she thought—the size of him, the feel of him, his clever fingers, his even cleverer tongue.

She was wet again just thinking about it. Which was insane. Crazy. Wild.

But if last night had taught her anything, it was that those three things weren't anything to be afraid of, and that losing control every now and then was exactly what she needed.

Lucas was still asleep, she noted a little wistfully. She wanted to wake him, preferably by sliding on top of him and taking him inside her again, but she wasn't sure her newfound sense of daring extended to multiple acts of man-jumping. Yesterday, she had been determined to start living and stop hiding when she strode into his room and asked for what she wanted, but it still hadn't stopped her from being afraid. There had been a moment there, right before instinct took over from everything else, when her fear of losing control had washed over her again. But she had ridden it out. And it had been worth it. A whole new world had opened to her, taught her things about herself that amazed her. Like that she could enjoy having a man in her mouth so much. He had tasted so good, and the power she'd felt as his body had tightened like a bowstring as he neared his climax… It had been an enormous turn-on.

Sex had never been like that with Brandon. But, after last night, she had a list as long as her arm of things that had never been like that with Brandon.

She really *had* been living half a life, sacrificing joy and excitement and feeling alive for safety and familiarity and the known. She felt a momentary sadness when she thought of Brandon. Had it been the same for him, too? Was he sitting somewhere right now, thinking about all the years they'd played it safe with each other?

Feeling the sudden need to be outside, she eased from the bed, found her clothes, and tiptoed into the hall to get dressed. Making her way downstairs, she slipped silently across the living room and eased the terrace door open. Across the terrace, down past the pool…she hesitated for a moment by the blue water, then stepped closer to the edge and dipped a toe in. Without thinking, she closed her eyes and let her body simply fall, slack and loose, into the water, clothes and all.

The warm water embraced her as she sank, and she lay on the bottom for a few precious seconds and stared up at the surface of the water, marveling at the way the light rippled through the blue.

Breaking the surface, she swam toward the broad steps and waded up them until she was half out of the water. Sitting, she leaned against the next highest step, the water lapping around her chest, and closed her eyes.

With the morning sun warming her face, Sophie made a conscious effort to remember the good times with Brandon. At the very least, he had been her best, closest friend for fourteen years. They had laughed, and cried and fought and loved with each other. She would be doing both of them a disservice if she filed their relationship under Regret.

Sucking in a great big breath, she let it out on a belly-deep sigh, consciously letting go of the past at the same time. Today, this morning, was her new beginning. Lucas had allowed her to unlock parts of herself last night. Now, it was up to her to rise to the challenge of ensuring that she continued to resist the urge to play it safe, to subvert her true desires, to live in fear.

Opening her eyes, she chased clouds across the blue, blue sky and let her mind range over the possibilities and choices that lay ahead for her. For starters, she needed a new job. That was a given, of course, with her awkward relationship with Brandon. As much as she loved his family, and they loved her, it would be uncomfortable for all of them if she stayed at Sorrentino's. Plus, she'd worked there since she'd left culinary school. She'd never known any other kitchen. The thought of branching out into a new style of cooking was as exciting as it was scary. But she was going to do it. And maybe not necessarily here in Australia, either, she suddenly decided. Maybe she'd try her luck in London, or even Europe. Why the hell not?

Despite her bravado, her stomach knotted with tension as she thought about the kinds of risks she'd be taking professionally and personally. Leaving her family and friends, everything familiar and comfortable.

"Stuff it," she said out loud. Deliberately, she remembered Mrs. Hartley's roses, and the fierce indignation and fearlessness that had driven her to wreak revenge on their busybody old neighbor. Once, she had been brave, larger than life.

She could be that way again. And she owed it to Carrie to try, she suddenly realized. Living half a life would not bring her sister back or stop Sophie from feeling pain and loss in the future.

Closing her eyes again, she dropped her head back and allowed herself to dream....

8

LUCAS WOKE TO A FEELING of utter well-being—until he remembered why his body felt so loose and well-used. Sex with Sophie Gallagher. Bone-jarring, teeth-grinding, hot-tamale sex. Sex that he would never have again once he said what needed to be said this morning.

Damn it.

It was tempting to say to hell with the consequences and continue sleeping with her. But he'd already acknowledged that Sophie wasn't like the women he usually bedded. He would hurt her if he took what he wanted for as long as he fancied it, as he had hurt other women before he'd learned that it was best to keep things light, limit himself to a couple of nights or a handful of days then move on to the next eager woman who knew the score.

So now he had to give Sophie the what's-what speech. The one where he told her that last night had been great, but that it was a one-off. Like that wasn't going to be one awkward, son-of-a-bitch conversation.

He heard her before he saw her—she was humming, something poppy and catchy. When he rounded the corner into the kitchen, he saw that she was dancing, too, her derriere wiggling as she boogied from the fridge to the counter.

"Good morning," she said when she saw him. She smiled, her face open and sunny.

Man, he felt like he was about to kick a puppy.

Do it. Get it over and done with.

Right. He took a deep breath. Then let it out again. After breakfast. He'd do it after breakfast. Definitely.

"You know, this diet you're on really sucks," she said as she arranged fruit salad and yet more cottage cheese on a plate for him. "I could make you a nice egg-white omelet, or even some homemade beans that would be just as good for you."

His mouth watered, and he wasn't sure if it was because she was wearing a tight black tank top or because her alternative menu suggestions sounded so good.

"Thanks, but I'd better stick to the stupid thing," he said. Just like he had to stick to his decision to let her know the score. Regardless of how reluctant he felt to do that now that she was smiling at him so warmly.

"Do you mind if I eat with you?" she asked.

She'd arranged another plate for herself, but he saw she'd added some slices of fruit bread to her meal in lieu of the cheese. If only. He coveted the bread, remembering fondly the days when carbs had been his friends. Was it really only three days ago?

"Sure," he said. "That'd be…nice."

She carried their plates to the table since it was difficult for him to use his crutches and carry a plate at the same time.

Once they were both seated, she picked up a piece of apple and popped it in her mouth.

"Listen," she said in between crunching on the fruit, "I wanted to thank you again for last night. It was great." She was blushing, but her gaze was determined as she eyed him across the table.

Shit. Things were about to get awkward.

Do it, he ordered himself. *Look in her big cinnamon eyes and be the cold bastard you know you are.*

He cleared his throat and shifted in his chair. Man, this was harder than he thought it would be.

"Sophie," he finally said. Then he ran out of words.

She waited a beat, and when he didn't say anything else, she cocked an eyebrow at him in inquiry.

"Lucas," she said, mimicking him.

He couldn't help himself—he smiled. Catching himself, he firmed his mouth and tried again.

"Sophie, like you said, last night was great. Really great."

Especially the shower. The way she'd—

"Anyway. I just thought we should clarify where we both stand," he said, cutting his own thoughts off ruthlessly. "I didn't want either of us to misconstrue anything that was said or done, or to give any of it more meaning than it necessarily had."

She was frowning in concentration, as though she was trying to work out what he was saying.

He cleared his throat again. "For some women, I know, sex is more than just sex. But my work commitments mean that taking anything beyond the casual is not practical."

She was staring at him, an incredulous expression on her face. Then she threw back her head and laughed, a loud, raucous crack that echoed around the living room.

"Lucas," she finally said, "are you warning me off?"

Suddenly he was feeling a little foolish, and he wasn't quite sure why.

"I don't want either of us to be under any illusions about what last night was about. I am not a one-woman kind of guy. Never have been, never will be."

She was shaking her head in disbelief. "Are you telling me that there are women out there who actually think that you're a white-picket-fence and two-point-five-kids kind of guy? Seriously?" she asked.

"I've had my fair share of tearful scenes, if that's what you mean," he said. For some reason he was feeling a little defensive.

"*Unbelievable.* Have they never read a magazine in their lives? You're like the poster boy for partying. You and Colin Farrell and Tommy Lee. I can't believe that any woman could delude herself into thinking that you would ever settle down. Talk about willful self-deception."

Still shaking her head, she grabbed another piece of apple. "You not hungry?" she asked, indicating his plate.

"No. I mean, yes," he said, absently shoveling a spoonful of cottage cheese into his mouth before he'd realized what he'd done. While he swallowed it like a kid taking cod liver oil, Sophie bit into her fruit bread. He had the sudden urge to snatch the slice from her hand and throw it across the room. And not just because she could eat carbs and he couldn't.

He was, he admitted, disgruntled. Which was madness in the extreme. Last night, he'd had eye-popping sex with a woman who had surprised and aroused him at every turn. And this morning, she'd let him know in no uncertain terms that, contrary to his concerns, the whole experience had been as mindless, shallow and meaningless as every other casual sexual encounter he'd ever had in his life.

He should be sitting back and blessing his lucky escape from what could have been an uncomfortable, messy scene.

But somehow, he wasn't.

SOPHIE COULDN'T HELP thinking about Lucas's little post-coital clarification chat as she cleaned up after breakfast. The image of him squirming in his chair as he tried to work around to his point was priceless, and something she would get a kick out of for some time to come. But she was still bemused by the fact that there were women in the world who looked at a man like him and truly believed he could be domesticated.

She made a disbelieving sound as she wiped down the counter. Were there any limits to the romantic fantasies women could convince themselves to believe in? Although, thinking about it objectively, she supposed she could *almost* understand how a woman could allow herself to be seduced into believing Lucas's intense love-making and easy charm meant more than it did. The same qualities that made him so watchable on the big screen ensured that spending time with him was exciting, exhilarating, addictive. But the man was a playboy, all about fun and instant gratification. Not exactly great happy-ever-after material. Hell, he probably wasn't even a good bet for happy-this-time-next-week. And the woman who allowed herself to believe any differently was setting herself up for a fall indeed.

He was, however, perfect material for a once-in-a-lifetime sensual experience. In fact, she couldn't think of a better candidate for what had happened between them last night. Hot body, great lover, endless stamina—he'd been exactly what she'd needed to shuck off the past in spectacular, splashy style. Oh, yeah.

Closing her eyes for a second, she relived that first slide of his body inside hers. He'd been so hard, so big, and she'd been so ready for him. She smiled as she remembered the way his amazing amber eyes had run appreciatively over her body, the satisfied grunt he'd made when he cupped her butt in his hands and pulled her more tightly against him.

He'd provided her with enough erotic material to fuel a thousand future fantasies. It was a pity that she wasn't going to have a chance to collect a few more. He was so good, it had been so hot between them. Even just one more night...

Sophie straightened abruptly as she clued in to what she was doing—yearning for more of Lucas Grant.

That way, she knew absolutely, lay stupidity. Hadn't she just been shaking her head over women who allowed themselves to believe that a man like him could be tamed? Wanting another night with him was simply the first step down a slippery slope that led inevitably to that kind of self-delusion. She was too smart and too self-aware to let herself fall in that trap.

Feeling more than a little smug at her ability to walk away from one of the world's most notorious woman- izers with a satisfied smile on her face and no regrets, Sophie headed back to the cottage.

She was at loose ends until it was time to prepare Lucas's lunch. She could swim. Or borrow a book from the library in the main house…. Wandering through her living room, her gaze fell on the jumbled pile of recipe books she'd brought with her, packed during those crazy few hours after Brandon's announcement.

Perfect. Nothing better than a little food porn to kill an hour or two.

Selecting a couple of books, she made her way outside and planted herself on a lounger at the shady end of the pool closest to the house.

Vaguely she wondered where Lucas had gone as she opened the first book. She acknowledged that she'd enjoyed having him flirt and pursue her over the past few days. What woman wouldn't, after all?

Stop thinking about him, idiot, she warned herself. *He is not the center of the universe, even if certain unruly body parts beg to differ.*

Forcing herself to focus, she leafed through the book, admiring the pictures, stopping to read an occasional recipe in detail. After twenty minutes, she was feeling pleasantly dozy. She'd only had a few hours' sleep last night, so she adjusted the back on her lounger to the prone position and closed her eyes.

Images from the recipe book drifted across her mind as her body relaxed. The bright red of tomatoes, the rich purple of eggplants, the crisp green of fresh peas.

Golden pie crusts, sugar-sprinkled pastries, floury handmade pastas. Almost without her controlling it, her mind began to make connections. For years she'd served a ravioli appetizer at Sorrentino's, filled with a mild ricotta and spinach blend, served with a fresh tomato coulis.

This morning, she imagined something different. What if, instead of making a handful of smaller raviolis, she made a single, more substantial one— elegant and simple? And what if she complemented that elegance and simplicity with the most simple filling of all—an egg yolk, cooked until it was warm and runny? She could serve it with buttered Italian bread— No! Toasted brioche—and a swirl of truffle oil. She laughed out loud at how quirky the combination would be.

Even though she had no idea what menu she was planning, or if she would ever turn these ideas into real creations, Sophie allowed herself to imagine an entrée to follow her appetizer.

Tender lamb, perhaps. Served in small, cylindrical portions—tornadoes—and rolled in goat cheese. She could serve it with mushrooms. Creamy, frothy mushrooms…like a parfait, but savory. Well, why not a parfait? A mushroom parfait. She was making this up as she went along, after all. Thinking outside the recipe.

Next, something rich to support the creaminess of the parfait and the bite of the goat cheese and the flavor of the lamb. Olives? A tapenade, maybe? She screwed up her nose, unhappy with such a conventional accompaniment when the rest of her fantasy menu was so outlandish. So…what if it was some kind of olive pâté? Or… Sophie laughed out loud again and clapped her hands together with delight at her own outrageous thought.

What if it was an olive *sorbet?* She'd imagined a savory parfait, why not a savory sorbet? Yes. Definitely. The combination of hot and cold, the textures, the flavors… Her fingers itched to pick up a knife and get started.

Now dessert—

"What the hell is this?"

Lucas's voice was so explosively angry and so close that Sophie started. Opening her eyes, she fully expected to find him standing over her, but he was nowhere to be seen.

"I expressly told you that my patronage was to remain confidential and anonymous. Which part of that didn't you get?" Lucas said.

Peering around the edge of her chair, Sophie saw she was lying near the open French doors to the library. She'd taken herself on a quick tour of the ground floor the first night she'd arrived, and she knew the room boasted a formidable collection of books, two desks and a state-of-the-art computer and communications system. She could see Lucas behind one of the desks, his crutches leaning against the wall behind him. Even at a distance she could recognize the tension in his body.

"No. That's not what we discussed. That's not part of the deal," Lucas said.

He swore angrily, clearly not hearing what he wanted from his caller.

"It's not negotiable, Derek. Talk to St. Barnaby's and explain the situation. It's your mess, you fix it," he snapped.

She was eavesdropping. She had the distinct impression that Lucas wouldn't appreciate her overhearing his conversation, not when he was throwing words like *confidentiality* and *anonymity* around. Easing out of the lounger, she aimed for a quick getaway.

Unfortunately, she'd barely got both feet on the ground and started to stand when Lucas came barreling out of the French doors.

LUCAS STOPPED in his tracks when he saw her.

He was distinctly pissy, mostly because he wanted to kick Derek's ass in person and he'd had to make do with a phone call. Which she'd probably heard most of.

"Everything okay?" she asked, confirming his suspicion.

Not that he particularly cared what she thought of him, but he could imagine how bad his rant must have sounded from her end.

"My manager and I are having a difference of opinion."

"Right."

He didn't owe her an explanation. Far from it. He should move on and forget about it.

Tossing his crutches to one side, he dropped onto the lounger next to where she stood. "It's not like I don't give him everything he needs to do his job. I go to opening nights, I do press interviews. Bloody hell, I did that stupid centerfold for *Cosmopolitan* last year. My arrangement with St. Barnaby's was not up for grabs, and he knew it. But he still had to try to squeeze something out of it, anyway."

Sophie was frowning, trying to decipher his stream-of-consciousness venting.

"St. Barnaby's is…?" she asked.

He glared at the brace on his knee. "A charity. They make sure that kids without parents don't have to miss out on everything in life."

"Do they want more money or something?" she asked.

He flicked her a look. Money he had plenty of.

"No. They want to nominate me for a humanitarian award." Just saying it out loud made him grind his teeth.

"You don't want them to?" She sounded surprised.

"They're not supposed to even know who I am. I made that clear to Derek when I signed on with him three years ago. That's the way it's always been. But Derek couldn't leave it—one sniff of a publicity opportunity, and he's like a dog in heat. So he tells St. Barnaby's who I am, and the next thing I know they've put me up for this award."

Reciting the situation pissed him off all over again. He really was going to kick Derek's ass when he got back to Sydney. Some things in his life were nonnegotiable, and his involvement with St. Barnaby's was one of them.

"Most people would be pretty happy to get an award telling the world they're nice to disadvantaged kids," Sophie said.

Lucas frowned at her. "Then they're egotistical jerk-offs. I don't donate for recognition or pats on the back. It needs to be done, that's all. People shouldn't be rewarded for doing the decent thing."

"Okay." She said it neutrally, but he knew he'd spoken too harshly.

"Sorry. Derek's the one I should be yelling at."

"I might be missing something really fundamental here, but doesn't he work for you? Shouldn't he do what you want him to do? Respect your wishes?"

"Derek's always been a total slut for publicity. He'd have me on the cover of something every week if he could," Lucas said, rubbing the bridge of his nose wearily.

In all honesty, now that he'd thought about it, he was surprised Derek hadn't done this earlier. In fact, it was practically a miracle he'd let the arrangement continue for three years.

Damn it. No matter how Lucas looked at it, the cat was out of the bag. Even if Derek could have him withdrawn from the award nomination, the staff at St. Barnaby's now knew who their mystery benefactor was. It would only be a matter of time before the press got wind of it.

Bloody Derek.

Pushing himself to his feet again, he grabbed his crutches. He needed to clear his head, get out of this place for a few hours.

"Listen, I'm going to go for a drive," he said to Sophie. "I might not be back for lunch."

"Okay."

He hesitated a beat.

"You want to come?"

There was a surprised silence as his question hung between them. He hadn't known he was going to say that. What was with his impulse control lately? And why was he so keen to spend time with her, now that he'd had her?

Sure, the sex had been incredible. Really, really good. But their conversation this morning had pretty much drawn a line under anything further happening. After all, he was the one who'd made the big song and dance about it being a one-off.

He wasn't quite sure why, now. Especially when he let his gaze drop to her breasts and he remembered how heavy and sweet they'd felt in his hands.

"Why not?" she said.

Despite his irritation with Derek, he couldn't help but smile. There were about a million women on three continents who would leap across a flame-filled canyon to come for a drive with him—but not Ms. Sophie Gallagher, apparently.

"Give me a second to grab my purse," she said.

She was back in two minutes sporting a pair of enormous Jackie O-style sunglasses and carrying a neat black purse.

"I hope you've got a big expensive penis car," she said conversationally. "I'll be really disappointed if you haven't."

"A penis car?"

"Yeah, you know—a phallic symbol on wheels that has been expressly designed to reassure a man of his virility and, ahem, stature. Not that you need any help in that department."

"Flattery will get you everywhere, Ms. Gallagher," he said, leading her across the terrace toward the garage.

"Says the man with the biggest dick in Hollywood," she said.

He stopped so abruptly that she almost walked into him. "Excuse me?"

When he turned to face her, frowning, she raised her eyebrows in amused incredulity. "Don't tell me you don't know?"

He just stared at her.

"How can you hold a title like that and not know?" she asked.

"It's not a topic that comes up a lot with my neighbors and colleagues," he said. To be honest, he wasn't sure if he was pleased or disturbed. To his utter surprise, he also realized he was blushing.

He couldn't remember the last time he'd blushed. If he'd *ever* blushed, in fact.

Sophie's amusement turned to admiration when they entered the Jenkinses' four-car garage and she spotted his gunmetal-gray Porsche Boxster convertible.

"Wow. Nice," she said. "My dad always dreamed of having one of these."

She ran a hand over the paintwork, leaning forward to admire the sleek black dash and leather interior. It had been a while since he'd seen his toys through someone else's eyes. It was a beautiful car—he simply hadn't seen it that way for a while.

"Here," he said, tossing her the keys. "You drive."

Her response was immediate and unequivocal. "Oh, no. I couldn't," she said firmly, handing the keys straight back to him.

"Why not?"

"No. Something might happen," she said, looking very prim all of a sudden.

He shrugged. It was no skin off his nose, after all. But he was aware of feeling vaguely disappointed. She'd seemed to get off on the car, and he'd thought driving it would be a buzz for her.

Tucking his crutches in the small cargo space behind the seats, he climbed in and waited till she'd fastened her seat belt before reversing out of the garage. She frowned intensely behind her big sunglasses and chewed on her full bottom lip all the while. Just as he was about to swing around and start down the driveway, she turned to face him.

"Um. If it's not too late, I think I would like to drive," she said in a rush.

He raised his eyebrows but didn't question her change of heart. "Sure."

She broke into a nervous smile. "Cool."

It took them a few minutes to exit the car and change sides. He couldn't help laughing when he saw how much distance there was between her and the pedals with the seat still set for his height.

"Adjustment's to the right," he said, watching as she scooted about as close to the steering wheel as she could get without wearing the damn thing.

"How tall are you, exactly?" he asked.

"Five foot two and a quarter inches," she said.

"And a quarter?"

"Believe me, every bit counts when your ass is this close to the ground," she said.

Right on cue, he had a quick flash of that very same ass wiggling its way into his bathroom last night.

"So, how does this thing work?" she asked, gesturing toward the tiptronic gear controls on the Porsche's steering wheel.

Dragging his mind out of her underwear, Lucas explained that, like a race car, it allowed the driver to either shift conventionally using clutch and gear stick, or using the steering wheel controls alone to work the gears.

"Okay, I think I get it," she said. "Here goes."

She accelerated slowly away from the house. She was concentrating fiercely, he was amused to see, even though they were only doing about five miles an hour.

"Careful, I think we overtook a turtle back there," he said.

She shot him a challenging look. "You want me to go faster?" she asked.

"Sure. Why the hell not?"

Her hands gripped the steering wheel, and he could feel the tension in her body, but she shifted a gear and put her foot down.

"This all you got?" he taunted as she turned left out of the driveway, enjoying watching her test herself.

She didn't even look at him this time as she changed another gear and the car surged forward with a burst of speed. Suddenly there was wind in his hair and the world was flashing past in a blur of color.

"I feel like James Bond," she said as she took a corner at speed, her cheeks flushed. Then she laughed. "A really, really nervous James Bond."

"Little Jimmy Bond," he suggested, and for some reason they both found that incredibly funny.

"You're a good driver," he observed after a while. "Confident, but not too cocky."

"Yeah?" She flashed a pleased smile at him.

After twenty minutes of winding roads they drove into a picturesque mountain village lined with well-maintained heritage shopfronts. She stopped to check out the local bookshop, and after an initial hesitation he followed her inside. He was wearing his sunglasses, but it didn't take long for the first person to approach and ask for his autograph. Once he'd signed one, the sluice gates were open and soon he was surrounded by people offering T-shirts, diaries, even business cards for him to sign.

Sophie stood to one side, her expression growing darker as the minutes ticked by. Finally she stepped forward and insisted that Mr. Grant needed to get back to his hospital bed.

Hard for anyone to object to that, given his crutches and elaborate ankle and knee braces.

"Is it always like that?" she asked as they drove back to the house.

"Worse, usually. At my Sydney place, one paparazzi set up a taping device outside my house so he could record my cell phone conversations. And another bozo tried to scale the wall."

He said it matter-of-factly because being sought after by fans and photographers was part of the pact he'd entered into when he became an actor. He might only seek the public's adoration and approval when he was on stage or in the movie theater, but it was unrealistic to expect it not to spill over into the real world.

"That's outrageous," Sophie said hotly. "You deserve a private life like anyone else. It's not like you sold the rights to everything when you agreed to appear in a movie."

He shrugged. "The reality is the studios cultivate it. Big headlines and lots of press means good box office. Star watching is an industry, just like anything else. Maps to stars' homes, paparazzi packs, manufactured headlines—if people weren't interested, it would all die overnight. It only exists to feed the public's desire to know more."

"Then people need to learn to mind their own business," Sophie said staunchly.

"Good luck with that one," he said drily. "Remember the Inquisition? The Salem Witch Trials? People have been minding other people's business for as long as there have been communities."

"It doesn't make it right," she said stubbornly.

He glanced across at her, amused by the pugnacious tilt to her chin. It was kind of nice having someone in his corner who wasn't being paid to be there. There hadn't been a whole lot of people who'd put themselves out for him in his lifetime—until he'd become rich and famous, that is. Then people fell all over themselves to be of service.

But Sophie was different. She hadn't fallen into his arms when he cocked his little finger in her direction. And when she had come to his bed, it had been because she wanted him, and only him—not his fame, not his reputation, not his connections or some other nebulous thing.

Craving something he didn't even have a name for, Lucas glanced across at her. She was flicking her gaze between the road ahead and the stereo system, and as he watched she reached out and punched the power button.

An old Tears for Fears track blared out of the speakers, and she cranked the volume up.

"I love this song," she yelled over the music.

Then she started to sing—the worst, most out-of-tune caterwauling he'd ever heard in his life. She should have looked ridiculous. But she didn't. She looked... real. And warm. And infinitely sexy.

He wanted her again. Who was he kidding? He'd wanted her again this morning, even while he was giving her the brush-off. He'd wanted her when he asked her to come for a drive.

More and more, she called to him. He wanted to lose himself in her intensity and her honesty and her naturalness. He glanced across at her. She was wearing a tight black tank top and orange flip skirt that sat just above her knees. If he reached out right now, he could slide a hand beneath that skirt and up her thigh and be touching the heat of her in seconds. He could tease her through the silk of her underwear, feel her become wet with wanting....

His cock hardened in his jeans as he imagined her spreading her legs for him, inviting him in. He'd stroke her and stroke her until he pushed her over the edge and she cried out the way she had last night when she'd given in to her desire.

If only he hadn't drawn that stupid freakin' line in the sand this morning.

Screw it.

She'd enjoyed herself last night, that had been abundantly clear. Why wouldn't she want more, just as he did? He could eat a little humble pie on the whole "this is a one-off thing" if it meant tasting her again. Absolutely he could, given how much he wanted to be inside her again.

The car bounced as Sophie turned into the driveway of the estate, and Lucas prepared to make her an offer she couldn't refuse.

"I was just thinking," she said before he could open his mouth.

"Yes?"

Her hands were tight on the steering wheel again, he noticed.

"Last night was good, right?"

He gave her his absolute, full attention. "Yes." He had a feeling she was about to surprise him again.

"So, um, if we both were agreed that there were no strings attached, there'd be no reason why we couldn't do it again. Don't you think? Have sex, I mean."

His hard-on throbbed in earnest agreement as the rest of him responded to the nervous charm of her approach. "Definitely."

She shot him a questioning look. "Definitely we could?" she clarified.

"Yes," he said.

She smiled, a slow, mysterious, thoughtful little smile, and he knew she was remembering something from last night. Something good and hot and wild. Maybe his hands on her, or his tongue on her, or him hard inside her. It didn't matter—the important thing was that they'd just given themselves permission to enjoy each other again and they were about to make a whole new set of steamy memories.

She pulled in to the garage and turned the car off. For a moment they both sat in the car. Her breathing was a little fast.

She was excited. He was hard. Sounded like a perfect match to him.

"Before we do this," he said, his conscience riding his ass, "let's be very clear about what this is. I don't believe in love and marriage and happy-ever-after." His eyes held hers, making sure she got his message loud and clear. "We're here together for four weeks, give or take a few days. You're single, I'm single. We have amazing chemistry. That's all that this is about. Agreed?"

"Agreed," she said. She even held out her hand so they could shake on it.

He took her hand, shook it, then lifted it and pressed a kiss into her palm.

"Now get out of the car and take your panties off," he said.

He half expected her to say something, but she didn't. She simply slid her hand from his grasp, got out of the car, tossed her sunglasses onto the seat and held his eye while she lifted up her skirt and hooked her thumbs into her panties. Then she pulled them off and dropped them on top of her sunglasses. He spared them a glance, taking in the black silk and lace. Nice, but not as nice as Sophie's bare skin.

She started to walk around to his side of the car, but he shook his head.

"I want you on the hood," he said. Then he grinned, leaving her in no doubt as to what he intended.

By the time he'd exited the car and joined her, she

was perched on the edge of the hood, knees together, cheeks flushed.

"Comfortable?" he asked her.

She cocked her head to one side, considering.

"The metal's nice and warm from the engine." Her eyes were smoky with anticipation, her nipples already aroused.

"Hmm," he said, placing his hands on her knees.

Leaning forward to kiss her, he slid his hands slowly up her legs, sliding them apart as he went, his thumbs gliding up the smooth skin of her inner thighs until he stopped just short of the heart of her.

Breaking the kiss, he nuzzled her neck, his thumbs tracing small circles against her tender flesh.

"Lie back," he said.

He could feel her trembling. He was hard as rock. But he wanted to taste her.

Slowly she lowered herself. He took a moment to appreciate the picture she made before he moved in: thighs spread, eyes languid, her palms spread flat on the hood of his expensive sports car.

"What is it about hot women and fast cars?" he murmured as he braced his good knee against the fender, took the rest of his weight on one forearm braced flat against the hood and took a good, long look at her sex.

She was pretty and pink, delicate and mysterious, and he ducked his head to press a first kiss against her mound. Her hips jerked, and he smiled against her.

"Buckle up, baby, it's going to be a bumpy ride," he said.

And then he went to work.

I AM GOING TO DIE. This is too good. Too intense. I can't possibly survive this.

No one had ever gone downtown like it. He was so focused, so gentle yet firm. His tongue was incredibly hot and deliciously textured and when he sucked her into his mouth and flicked her again and again, she almost flew right off the car. Then he slid a finger inside her and the need coiled tighter and tighter.

"Oh. Yes!" Someone moaned really loudly, and she realized it was her. But she was so far beyond caring. All she wanted, needed, had to have was satisfaction.

He deepened his intimate kisses, sliding another finger inside her. She sobbed and lifted her hips and thrashed her head from side to side. He began to work his fingers inside her, his tongue all the time teasing her, pleasing her.

She felt her climax approaching like a tsunami, welling up, building from her toes until her whole body was tight with tension and her hands were fisted and her head thrown back as she cried out.

Then she came, her muscles tightening around his clever fingers, her thighs trembling with the force of it.

Afterward he kissed her thighs, her belly, her breasts before he took her mouth her again. He smelled of her sex, and even though she was boneless with satisfaction, she felt her hunger build again when she felt how hard he was through his jeans.

There was no question of him taking her on the hood, however, not with his injured knee. He pulled back from her with a reluctant groan.

"We need to go inside, now," he said.

"Yes," she said.

They made it to one of the loungers. He pulled her onto his lap, and she had him out of his jeans, protected and inside her within seconds. She'd expected him to want to go fast, but when she began to ride him hard, he pulled her close and pressed long, slow kisses against her neck, guiding their rhythm with his hands on her hips. Slow and languid, leisurely, savoring ever slide, every thrust, every withdrawal. She closed her eyes and clenched herself tight around him, feeling every inch of him, relishing the sweet friction.

By slow stages, the muscles of his back and shoulders hardened as he drew closer and closer to his own climax. Hers came suddenly, a swift, unexpected gift that had her shuddering in his arms as he thrust the last time deep into her, his face buried in her neck.

In that brief moment, she had a sudden flash of just how risky it was going to be for her to sleep with this man over the coming weeks. She already knew he had charisma and physical appeal to spare. He'd charmed her from day one, despite her best intentions and her fear of letting go. But it would be a mistake to dismiss her reaction to his appeal as merely physical.

She liked him. He was an unrepentant womanizer, a hard-drinking hell-raiser and a whole bunch of other things that should have been a lot less attractive than they were. Still she liked him. Hearing him talk about the price of fame and learning about his anonymous support of St. Barnaby's had been like catching a peek behind the curtain of the Great and All Powerful Oz and finding a real person instead of the cardboard-cutout Lucas presented at first glance.

Which made him so very dangerous to her.

But at the end of the day, her realization didn't make all that much difference, she knew. Because she wasn't going to say no to him. Not when her body craved his touch. Driving his car today, feeling him watching her, watching him in turn, getting hot for him all over again and knowing that one night had not been nearly enough…

Even though it was dangerous, she owed it to herself to have this experience. And she was damn well going to take it, for as long as it lasted.

9

LUCAS WOKE WITH A START, his body once again covered in sweat, his muscles bunched tight with the need to flee. For a moment he didn't know where he was. Then he registered Sophie's cool hands on his shoulders. Right. Sophie. The Jenkinses' Blue Mountain estate.

"Are you okay?" she asked, her small hands kneading his shoulders.

He'd had the nightmare again.

Shit.

It was bad enough that they'd started recurring in the first place, but that Sophie had to witness one… He might as well have wet the bed.

Pulling away from her, he swung his legs toward the floor and sat on the edge of the bed. His heart was still pounding, and he ran a shaky hand through his hair.

"Would you like a glass of water?" she asked after a long silence.

"I'm fine."

Levering himself to his feet, he grabbed his crutches and crossed to the bathroom. His reflection was nothing but a dark shadow in the minimal light, but he didn't flick the light on. He didn't particularly want to see himself right now.

After washing his face and gulping a glass of water, he returned to the bedroom. Sophie's side of the bed was still and silent, and he hoped that she'd gone back to sleep.

Hauling on his workout pants and a T-shirt, he made his way downstairs. The whiskey bottle called to him. He collected it and a glass, then made his way to the couch.

Was it just two days ago that he'd wound up taking refuge here? Maybe he should see a doctor, think about getting some sleeping pills or something. Whatever it took to banish the nightmare back to where it belonged—the past.

He'd just poured himself the first hit when Sophie joined him, her legs and arms pale against the dark fabric of one of his T-shirts. It reached midway down her thighs and looked far sexier than it had any right to, under the circumstances.

"Feel like company?" she asked.

He wanted to say no. Especially because he suspected she was about to get all Dr. Phil on his ass.

"Sure." He shrugged.

She crossed to the liquor cabinet, grabbed another glass, then walked barefoot across the floor to hand it to him.

"What are we drinking?" she asked as he poured for her.

"Whiskey. Irish, I think."

"Hmm." She took a sip and made a face.

"Don't like it?" he asked.

"To be honest, most grain liquor tastes like rubbing alcohol to me," she said, taking another sip. She sat in the armchair at right angles to the couch.

Here goes, he thought, bracing himself, *the well-intended questions.*

"You know, I'm pretty damn sure I saw a Scrabble board in those cabinets beside the fireplace the other day. Feel like playing?"

He stared at her.

"I'm going to take that as a yes," she said, getting up.

She riffled around in the Asian-style cabinets until she gave a victory cry.

"I should warn you, I used to play this all the time with my parents when I was a kid," she said.

Flicking on the nearest floor lamp, she sat cross-legged on the couch beside him and unfolded the board between them. After eyeing the alluring shadows beneath the hem of his T-shirt and speculating if she'd bothered with underwear, he watched with reluctant amusement as she organized the tiles face-down in the box and allocated them each a tile rack.

"Okay, a few guidelines. We're playing by Gallagher family rules, which means only words of a smutty, puerile or flat-out rude nature are allowed," she said briskly. "And I get to go first, because my family always let me or I would throw a tantrum." So saying, she gave her attention to her letters.

This was it? They were going to play a stupid board game? No amateur psychology? No attempts to comfort him?

"You want me to explain the rules again?" she asked, seeming to notice his stare for the first time.

"Nope. Got 'em," he said, at last dropping his gaze to his own tiles.

"Ooh, nice," she said suddenly, and he watched as she spelled out BOOBS on the board.

"You played this game with your parents?" he asked skeptically.

"Yep. And Mom always won, the dirty bitch. I guess being older she'd been around more than me and Carrie," Sophie said, extracting replacement tiles from the box. "Although I don't know what Dad's excuse was. Lack of imagination, I guess. Your turn."

He really didn't want to play, but she'd gone to a lot of trouble. The least he could do was stick a few words down before he bailed on her.

She nodded with approval when she saw his word: SHAG.

"Nice, and you got a triple word score there. Hmm." She rested her cheek on her hand as she contemplated her tiles. "Oh yeah, now I see it."

She spelled out BALLBAG, using his G as an end point. He nearly snorted whiskey out his nose in surprise. Maybe it was the alcohol kicking in, but he was starting to warm to this game.

Sophie frowned when she saw his next word: HAIRYOLA.

"What the hell is that?" she asked.

"A hairy areola. Hairyola for short," he said, poker-faced.

"That's a made-up word," she said.

"And *boobs* isn't? Just because it's not in the dictionary doesn't mean they don't exist."

She pulled a face. "Ew. More whiskey, please."

He topped her up, managing to get a decent look

down the loose neckline of her T-shirt when she leaned forward.

"No hairs down there, I think you'll find," she said archly as she took a sip of her drink.

"I know. But perhaps I should take a look, just in case," he suggested.

"Maybe we should make this a little more interesting and make it strip Scrabble," she countered.

As it wound up, he let her get one more word down before pulling her into his lap. Letter tiles flew everywhere as he stripped her naked.

"I was ahead on points. Just so we both know that," she said as he sucked one of her nipples into his mouth.

"I unreservedly conceded defeat," he said.

Afterward, she led him back to bed and curled against him. As he drifted back to sleep, he marveled at how she'd made him laugh and forget for a moment.

Every time she surprised him. Every damn time.

THE NEXT MORNING, Sophie woke before Lucas again and eased quietly out of bed. Collecting her clothes, she dressed outside the bedroom so as not to disturb him.

Last night when he woke shuddering and trembling beside her, her every instinct had screamed at her to take him in her arms and hold him. But she'd known without even trying that he wouldn't accept her comfort.

And why should he? They'd known each other for less than a week. They knew very little about each other's lives, apart from the very obvious stuff. Hell, she didn't even know his parents' names, where he grew up…none of the stuff she'd known about Brandon without ever having to ask. She and Lucas were two people who found mutual fulfillment in each other's arms, end of story.

Still, she hadn't been able to let him walk off into the night on his own. She'd remained in bed for a few minutes after he'd left, tossing up the options, wondering what sort of ghosts haunted him that his whole body had been so rigid. She'd gone after him and distracted him as best she could.

And just before she'd fallen asleep again, she'd had an idea. She wanted to do something for him. Something in lieu of comforting him.

Now, she had a quick shower, then went and did reconnaissance in the fridge. As she'd suspected, she had all the ingredients she needed there. Then she sat down with his diet chart and went to work.

By the time he joined her in the kitchen a couple of hours later, she'd roughed out a new program and was slicing herbs for his revamped breakfast.

"Hey. You're up early." He was a little subdued, she noted. Probably thinking about his nightmare, wishing she hadn't been there to witness it.

"I had something I wanted to take care of," she said. "I'll bring in your breakfast in a few minutes."

"I can hardly wait," he said drily. "Let me guess— today's special is cottage cheese."

She merely quirked an eyebrow at him, not wanting to give away her surprise.

Five minutes later she slid a savory-scented egg-white frittata filled with lean bacon, crunchy vegetables and fresh herbs, accompanied by chunky salsa, in front of him.

"You're kidding me. This is on my diet?" he asked.

"On your *new* diet chart," she said. Drawing her jottings from her back pocket, she spread them out in front of him. "I broke down the old plan into calorie counts and fat counts. Then I came up with a new menu that will keep you within the same boundaries, but allow you to actually enjoy your food, too."

He studied her workings for a moment. "No more cottage cheese?"

"No more cottage cheese."

He surveyed his plate as if he almost couldn't believe it was true. "This smells really good."

"Of course it does," she said with a complete absence of modesty. "It's real food. Whoever put that other diet together for you hates food."

She perched on the edge of the table, legs dangling, waiting for him to take his first mouthful.

He carved off a generous portion with his fork and carried it to his mouth. He closed his eyes, relishing the moment.

"What's the smoky flavor?" he asked once he'd swallowed.

"Smoked paprika. It's my favorite spice," she said. "You like it?"

"I love it," he said, attacking his plate with gusto.

She'd never gotten so much satisfaction out of watching someone eat. She felt mildly guilty, in fact, that she was enjoying herself so much when she'd supposedly done it for him.

"This is like culinary porn," she confessed as he pushed his plate away. "Cooking a meal then watching someone really get off on it. The ultimate payoff."

"Really?"

"Of course. Most of the time in a restaurant, you're so far away from the customers you have no idea if they like the meal or not. Sometimes they send their compliments, but mostly you figure that if they come back again and the dining room stays busy, you're doing okay."

He stood then, and she was about to slide off the table to start cleaning up when he stopped her with a hard, hot kiss.

"Thanks," he said. "I appreciate you going to the extra effort."

For some reason, his sincere gratitude made her feel very self-conscious and she could feel a blush stealing into her cheeks.

"It hurt me almost as much to prepare those meals as it hurt you to eat them," she said lightly.

"Mmm. I think we'll have to disagree on that one," he said drily.

Again she tried to slide off the table, and again he stopped her.

"Also," he said, "I wanted to say thanks for last night."

This time, he was the one who had trouble holding her eye.

"I didn't do anything," she said.

"You did, and you didn't. Thanks on both counts," he said.

Then he kissed her again, grabbed his crutches and was gone.

Sophie sat on the table for a moment longer, wondering. But it was none of her business. Big-time none of her business.

Lucas had another nightmare that night.

Sophie hadn't intended to stay in his bed again—their deal was sex, after all, not intimacy—but she'd dozed off after they'd come together for the second time. She woke to find his rigid body trembling beside her, his fists crushing the sheets as he fought an invisible demon.

As she had last night, she reached across and soothed his shoulders, trying to rouse him from the dream.

"Lucas. You're dreaming," she said gently but firmly. He awoke with a start, and she could feel his heart pounding hard where her palm was flat against his shoulder blade.

"Shit."

As he had last night, he rolled to the side of the bed and sat there, his elbows propped on his knees, his head in his hands. Wordless, she knelt behind him and tried to rub some of the tension out of his shoulders and neck. At first he remained stiff, resistant, but after a few minutes she felt him begin to let go.

"Do you want to talk about it?" she asked quietly.

He sighed, and she felt his shoulders tense again beneath her hands.

"It's just an old dream, nothing important."

"You know, sometimes just naming it helps. Puts a bit of perspective on it," she said.

He shifted restlessly, and she thought she'd pushed too hard. Fair enough. They didn't owe each other anything.

But then he started to talk, his voice low, almost inaudible.

"I'm just a kid. I have no idea how old. It's night, and

I'm on a bike, riding past an ordinary suburban house. It's not familiar to me, but I feel like it's mine, like it's home," he said.

She didn't say a word, simply stilled her hands on his shoulders and let him feel her touching him.

"All the windows and doors of the house are open, and the curtains are streaming out, as though there's a breeze inside pushing them out. The door is open, and I throw my bike down on the front lawn and race up the steps. Inside, the rooms are empty—no furniture, nothing except for pale marks on the wall where photographs and pictures should be. Everything is gone.

"I start running around the house, opening and shutting all the doors until I find the master bedroom. I throw the door open and rush inside, but there's only an empty bed…."

He trailed off. She blinked back tears for him. Like most dreams, the details of his nightmare sounded completely innocuous when spoken out loud, but she'd seen the effect it had on him.

"You were all alone," she said slowly. "Your family left you all alone."

He didn't say anything, but tension still vibrated through his body.

"I read a book on dream interpretation once," she said, trying to offer him something. "Houses in dreams are supposed to represent security, belonging, family. I think I'm getting this right. If it's a childhood home in your dream, one that you don't live in anymore, I think it's supposed to represent your desire for a family of your own. But I don't know what the open doors and windows mean. Or the empty rooms."

She wanted to help him so very badly. She'd wrestled with her own demons only very recently— was still wrestling with them, on some level, every time she let herself drive his car, or lie naked before him, or offer him the gift of a rude board game when he needed distraction.

He shifted again, huffed out a little laugh. "You know, it's probably because I moved around so much when I was a kid. I always wanted to stay in one place, but it never happened. Stupid."

There was a finality to his tone. The subject was closed. She got the message loud and clear. She moved back to her own side of the bed. After a beat, he laid down and pulled the sheet over himself.

Lying in the dark, facing away from him on her side, she fought the urge to turn around, curl against him and offer more comfort. But he didn't want anything more from her.

Remember the rules of engagement, Sophie. More importantly, remember those stupid women who believed in something that was never going to happen.

Too bad her vision of Lucas had shifted irrevocably over the past few days. He would never again be a shallow womanizer in her eyes, just a convenient body for her to get off on for a few hot weeks. He was a real and whole person—a vulnerable person, she was beginning to realize, despite all his apparent success and fame.

Behind her, the mattress dipped and she felt the warmth of his body as he moved closer to her. His arm snaked around her waist and he pulled her tight against him, his hips cradling her butt, his chest to her back.

Then she felt the press of his lips against the nape of her neck.

"Go to sleep, Sophie," he told her softly.

If the ridiculous warmth that washed through her weren't warning enough, the tears that burned at the back of her eyes were.

She was falling in serious like with Lucas Grant. Dangerous, indeed.

10

TWO WEEKS LATER, Lucas lounged beside the pool, the late-afternoon sun tamed by the umbrella shading his corner of the world. He hadn't had a single nightmare since he'd told Sophie his sad little tale, and neither of them had brought it up again. It was a nonissue, as far as he was concerned. He suspected Sophie felt otherwise, but she never raised it with him.

He glanced to where she was splashing around in the pool. She was doing a doggy paddle, her head held high. He couldn't help but smile.

A month ago, if anyone had told him that he'd be content to spend the bulk of every day with one person—someone he'd met recently, at that—he'd have laughed in their face. But Sophie was so easy, so warm, so genuine that each day was over before he knew it.

The sex helped a lot, of course. It seemed to get better and better. Now that they knew each other's hot spots, they could get one another crazy in a handful of seconds—or draw it out for hours on end. And in between the best sex of his life, they had fun.

Rude Scrabble had become a nightly challenge. He could only imagine what his party buddies in L.A.

would think of the fact that he actually looked forward to settling on the couch at night with only Sophie, a few inches of whiskey and all those stupid little tiles. At first he'd simply been humoring her, but pretty soon it had become a matter of pride to beat her. She had a dirty mind, and an even dirtier vocabulary, he'd quickly discovered. Commercial kitchens, she'd explained to him, were full of foul-mouthed, foul-tempered people under stress. Slowly he'd clawed ground back, however, and last night he'd won his first game.

They'd become friends, he realized. Physically intimate friends who liked each other's bodies one hell of a lot.

In the water, Sophie rolled onto her back and floated, the sweet peaks of her naked breasts breaking the surface of the water. He'd stolen her bikini top when he was in the water with her earlier, retaliation for an earlier bombing incident that had caught him full in the face. As he watched her appreciatively, a memory nudged at him—Candy-Cindy in a similar pose in his hot tub just a few weeks ago.

Two women could not be more different. Candy-Cindy had been all about artifice, seduction, ambition. Sophie was just Sophie. She had no agenda. It was amazing to him how refreshing that was.

God, he liked her. She was funny, smart, cheeky, challenging. Damned sexy. He was going to miss her when their four weeks were up.

Although just because they left the estate didn't necessarily mean he and Sophie had to stop seeing each other.

He frowned as the thought slipped into his mind. Where the hell had that come from? Then he decided to stop fooling himself—it had been hovering there for a while now, and he knew it. He just hadn't been prepared to own up to it yet.

He wasn't ready to let her go. And he wasn't quite sure how to deal with that. The odds were good that once he was back to his old life, his old routines, Sophie would quickly become a thing of the past, a pleasant memory of hot summer days and nights.

For some reason, even though the thought ought to have been comforting, it only made him feel uneasy.

Sitting up, he shaded his eyes so he could see her properly.

"Tired yet?" he called.

She stopped floating and stood in the shallow end of the pool, water sluicing off her curves as she pushed her hair out of her eyes.

"Sorry, what?" she asked.

"Are you ready to come out yet?" he asked, smiling faintly. She had no idea how hot she was, which was one of the things about her that drove him crazy. She was effortlessly sexy and sensual. And always, always responsive. His very own little auburn-haired fire cracker.

She lifted a shoulder in a casual shrug. "Sure. Why not?"

It was only when she exited the pool that he saw she'd shed her bikini bottom, as well. Poker-faced, she sauntered to the lounger where she'd left her towel.

"Mmm, the towel's all hot from the sun," she murmured as she blotted her face and hair dry. She eyed him from beneath her eyelashes as she rubbed the towel over her breasts, then lower, over her belly.

Predictably, he was hard in an instant, his erection tenting the damp fabric of his board shorts.

"Come here," he said.

She lifted a leg onto the lounger's arm and pretended to dry her thighs.

"Why?" she asked innocently.

"Sophie…" he growled, and she smirked and sauntered over, hips swinging.

"Yes, Mr. Grant?" she asked, stopping just outside his reach and pressing her upper arms to either side of her breasts so they sat up high, begging for his attention.

"Sophie, if I have to come after you, it's not going to be pretty," he warned her.

She pretended to give it some thought. "In that case…" And she strolled toward the house, giving him a mouthwatering view of her round, wiggling butt.

"Vixen," he said between his teeth, then he was on his feet and after her. She was almost at the house when she looked over her shoulder and saw he was advancing fast, and she picked up her pace. Not too much, since she wanted to be caught as much as he wanted to catch her. He ate up the ground with his crutches, gaining on her with every step. She was laughing when he finally tackled her on the stairs.

She rolled onto her back, her velvety eyes dark with passion. Then she looked into his face and she was suddenly very, very serious.

"Hurry," she said, sucking on her forefinger. He watched, mesmerized, as she traced the coral pink edge of a nipple with her damp finger. It pebbled hungrily under his avid gaze, and he stripped his board shorts off in record time.

"Go up a step," he ordered, and she used her arms to lift herself up to the next tread.

"And another," he repeated. She frowned, but still obeyed him.

"And one more," he said. He could see the flare of excitement in her eyes as she guessed what he intended. Her breath caught in her throat as he knelt on a lower step and pushed her legs apart.

Her head fell back on her neck as his hands swooped up the inside of her thighs. Gently, he probed her folds with his fingers, teasing her as he circled her clitoris, sliding in and out of her slick entrance, all the while watching the heart of her and the way her hips rose in invitation and pleading. She was so pretty. He loved doing this to her, watching her lose her mind. It was the biggest turn-on in the world.

"Lucas," she groaned, clenching and unclenching her hands.

"Just relax," he said. Then he lowered his head.

SOPHIE'S WHOLE BODY was shaking in response to what Lucas was doing between her thighs—tasting, sucking, biting, his tongue by turns urgent and demanding, then so delicate it made her want to scream.

She was so turned on, so aroused, she felt as though she was going to coalesce into a ball of need. Gripping the edge of the stair, she hung on for dear life and begged him to end it, to slide inside her and take them both to the place they wanted to be.

His response was to lift her legs onto his shoulders and deepen his exploration. She moaned low in her throat and reached for his head to anchor him there as she passed the point of no return and became nothing but greedy, demanding need.

He kept pace with her, using his hands now to tease her, as well, finally sliding one, two, then three fingers inside her. His tongue circled her clitoris, then he kissed her whole mound passionately with a hungry, openmouthed kiss, his tongue firm and knowing and demanding.

She fell apart. Her thighs trembled, and she spasmed around his fingers, her hips rising instinctively as she came and came and came. She barely registered the loss of his wet heat between her thighs, he moved so quickly. The next thing she knew, he was inside her and she was clutching his shoulders as he thrust powerfully into her.

Belatedly she realized he must have his weight on his bad knee. They'd been very careful for the past two weeks to always work around it, but now he was braced on it, hammering into her.

"Your knee," she reminded him.

He shrugged. "It doesn't hurt. That's good enough for me."

He kissed her, treating her mouth to the same thorough exploration her southern regions had just enjoyed. She surrendered herself utterly to the experience, powerless to do anything else. There was only his body, the feel of his skin beneath her hands, the slide of him inside her, the staccato counter-beat of their individual breaths, the thrust and flex of muscles as they strained toward fulfillment.

She closed her eyes as she felt herself rising again. He was thrusting fast and hard, lifting his hips higher to gain the most stimulation with each stroke, and she was calling out his name, clinging to him as he shuddered into her one last time, his whole body hard with demand as he rode his own climax.

He pressed his face into her neck briefly afterward, kissed her gently there, then he rolled to one side. For a few long minutes they both just reclined there on the stairs, naked, glistening with perspiration and desire, staring up at the vast open space above the stairwell.

"Now would be a really good time for Julia Jenkins to drop in for a surprise visit," Sophie said after a while.

Lucas laughed, the sound low and rewarding. She liked to make him laugh. It had become something of a mission for her over the past few weeks, in fact. He was so human and approachable when he was amused—his eyes bright, his head tilted slightly back and his body relaxed.

She glanced at him, her gaze skimming the strong lines of his profile. He was almost ridiculously good-looking, with his strong, straight nose, his cheekbones, those amber eyes. None of which gave any hint of the man beneath all the superficial attractiveness. The Lucas Grant she had been lucky enough to get to know was so much more than a collection of pleasing body parts and facial features. He appreciated good food in a way that gratified her chef's soul. He was also surprisingly courteous and considerate—surprisingly because she suspected he'd had his own wants catered to on an hourly basis for many years. But it hadn't turned him into an ego-driven monster, despite what she'd thought of him initially.

He was also generous, in so many ways. In the bedroom, he was the most lusty yet considerate lover she'd ever imagined. And then there was St. Barnaby's. From little things he'd said over the past few weeks, she'd worked out that he contributed to other charities, too, all of them for children. She suspected he did so anonymously, as with St. Barnaby's.

What kind of man didn't want the world to know he cared for something other than his own apparently hedonistic lifestyle? What kind of lessons had life thrown at him to make him so afraid to show his true self?

They were questions that sat in the back of her mind every day, but she knew she would never ask them.

Fun. They were all about fun.

She snapped out of her reverie as Lucas stretched and yawned beside her. "Is it nap time, Ms. Gallagher?" he asked.

"You're spoiling me, you know that, don't you? How am I supposed to go back to normal life after four weeks of so much laziness and decadence?"

"You've been doing your tinkering in the kitchen every afternoon. That's not decadent," he said.

She pulled a face. If he knew what she'd been tinkering with—her mushroom parfait and her olive sorbet and her poached-egg ravioli, experimenting and testing and adjusting until she got her recipes right—he might be inclined to retract his statement. It was pure indulgence. Still, she was quietly excited by some of the combinations she'd come up with.

She eyed him, wondering if it was time to test her new ideas on an audience yet. But her toes curled a little at the thought. What if it was all an abject failure? Lucas was the last person she wanted to witness her falling on her face.

She frowned, recognizing the thought for what it was—Old Sophie, once again desperately seeking a rational, safe foothold. For that reason alone she knew she should ask Lucas to be her first test audience. But she probably wouldn't. Her ideas were too new, too fragile and fantastic. And his opinion meant too much to her.

Talk about walking a fine line.

Again she gave herself the lecture that was practically her mantra: she'd be stupid to let the intimacy of the past few weeks fool her into believing that what was happening meant anything or was special or anything else equally deluded. Just because she had discovered the man behind the mask didn't mean anything. He was thirty-five years old and an avowed bachelor. He lived his life at full tilt. She must never forget those pictures of him in those magazines, the ones where he was drunk and partying with some leggy blonde. That was the life that awaited him outside the gates of this estate, the life he would be returning to.

Lucas ran his finger across her forehead, soothing the frown that had formed between her eyebrows.

"What's this for?" he asked.

"Nothing. Just thinking," she said dismissively.

He hesitated a moment, then reached for his crutches. "Bed calls," he said. "Come on."

We're in a bubble, she thought as she tilted her head back and watched him make his way up the stairs. *Two people high in the mountains, enjoying a time-out from the normal world.* Up here, they could pretend that they were equals, and that there was nothing beyond the next few hours to worry about. And it was true, too. For another two weeks, at least.

She stood to follow him, but was distracted by the ring of her cell phone. She'd left it on the dining room table, and she made her way down the stairs to collect it.

She'd never been particularly self-conscious about nudity or her body—apart from wishing for a few extra inches in height, all of it leg—but it was hard not to feel the slightest bit exposed wandering around this huge, luxurious house in her birthday suit. It was the kind of house that made a person feel really, really small, human and naked. Consequently, she returned to her perch on the stairs as she took the call.

"Sophie, it's me. I'm just ringing to see how you're doing," Becky said.

"Becks," Sophie said, delighted to hear from her friend. "How are you?"

"I'm good. You still okay up there?"

Sophie glanced down at her nudity. "Let's just say I'm enjoying myself," she said.

Becky sighed enviously. "Lucky girl. Lucky, lucky girl. I would kill to be in your shoes."

"How did your court case go?" Sophie asked, deliberately changing the subject. She hadn't mentioned a word about what was happening between her and Lucas. For starters, she knew he valued his privacy. While she didn't for a second think that Becky would blab to one of the tabloids or something equally revolting, Sophie still felt uncomfortable talking about him to anyone. This might just be about sex, but what was happening up here in the Blue Mountains was…private. Personal. About her and him, and the rest of the world be damned.

And, perhaps foolishly, there was a part of her that believed that if no one else knew, it wouldn't be quite so bad when she and Lucas finally said goodbye and went their separate ways.

Yeah, right.

"Actually, the reason I'm calling is because there's this new book coming out about Lucas. An unauthorized biography," Becky said. "Normally I wouldn't read one of those things, you know. They're so tacky. But there was an excerpt in the weekend paper and I couldn't resist."

Sophie stiffened, sure that Becky was about to start filling her in on lurid details from Lucas's past. She so didn't need to know which beautiful women Lucas had slept with before her. It wasn't jealousy or possessiveness, she assured herself, just peace of mind. Who wanted to be compared to Halle Berry, for example? Not Sophie. Not in a million years.

"You know what, Beck—"

"It's amazing how a person can look like they've got it all, but underneath they've missed out on so much," Becky said.

Sophie opened her mouth to protest again, but it was too late. She'd heard Becky's words and now she wanted to know exactly what Lucas had missed out on. For a second longer she warred with her conscience, but it was no match for her curiosity. Not when she'd witnessed Lucas's nightmares and sensed how badly something or someone had damaged him in the past.

"What did the article say?" she asked. She shot a glance over her shoulder, hating the thought of Lucas catching her talking about him.

"That he was a ward of the state who grew up in state homes. He was fostered out a number of times, but he never seemed to stick until he was in his teens. No one knows what happened to his parents, whether they died or dumped him or what—the reporter couldn't get access to Lucas's records," Becky said.

Sophie sucked in her breath. She felt as though someone had punched her in the belly. She flashed to that night Lucas had finally told her about his dream. His nightmare had been about an empty house and missing parents. No wonder.

"It sounds like this guy has dug around in Lucas's life enough already," Sophie said, starting to get angry on Lucas's behalf. She knew without asking that he would consider this book a massive invasion of his privacy. This wasn't a charity donation that was being made public, this was his pain. Pain he kept hidden even from himself.

"Yeah. There's a picture of the author with the article. He looks like a real jerk," Becky said. "Weaselly, if you know what I mean."

After they wound up their conversation Sophie sat in silence for a few minutes, her thoughts churning. Lucas was an orphan. He'd grown up without a home. She could only imagine what he'd gone through in his life. Had he been abandoned, or had something happened to his family? Had he been abused? God, had he ever been loved, the way all little boys should be loved?

He was sprawled across the center of the bed already asleep when she entered the bedroom. She stood watching him, feeling for him. He might be big and strong now, but once he'd been a little boy with no home and no one to tell him he was special. She was the product of two people who had loved each other and her sister unconditionally. She couldn't even begin to imagine how it would feel to be so alone in the world.

She felt like crying. She wanted to crawl into bed beside him and wrap her body around his to try to ease his hurts. Because he *was* hurt, broken in some way. She understood that now.

But it wasn't her place to care about him in that way, and she knew without a doubt that he would reject her tears and her empathy.

Dressing quietly, she made her way downstairs. She felt restless, a little sick in the stomach. So much for this being a sex-only fling. She'd passed the point of protecting herself long ago. She was with Lucas for the duration. Then she would start her new life without him. And he would go back to pretending he didn't care about anyone.

Without really thinking about it, she gravitated to the kitchen. The only currencies that he was prepared to accept from her were sex and food. So she would give him a culinary experience. And in doing that, she would give him something of herself, too. And maybe— No. That would be expecting too much from a man like Lucas. She squashed the thought before it was even fully formed. She would cook for him, invite him into her imagination. It would be a gift, just as making his diet bearable had been a gift. And that was *all* it would be.

11

SINCE HE'D BEEN BANNED from the kitchen for the bulk of the afternoon and early evening, Lucas knew that something was up. The bottle of wine on the table confirmed it, as did Sophie's first words when she entered from the kitchen, two plates in hand.

"Tonight's meal is going to be a little different," she said as she slid a plate in front of him.

He studied his meal: a single, rustic-looking ravioli, surrounded by a squiggle of dark olive-colored oil and flanked by two slices of buttered, oval-shaped bread. Saliva pooled in his mouth.

"It's not on your diet," she said a little defiantly. "But I wanted to show you what I've been working on."

"Screw the diet. This looks fantastic."

She was asking him to be her taste tester. For some reason, the thought gave him a warm feeling in his belly.

She sat opposite him, and waited for him to start first.

Palming his cutlery, he cut the corner off his ravioli. To his surprise, a warm, thick egg yolk oozed out.

"Cool," he said. Swirling a forkful of the pasta in the oil, he lifted it to his mouth.

Flavors danced across his tongue, simple but delicious. He moaned and Sophie smiled.

"You like it," she said.

"It's great. Delicious. What's this green stuff?" he asked, gesturing toward the oil.

"Truffle oil."

Then he tried a piece of the toast. It was buttery, decadently so.

"Brioche," she explained when he shot her a questioning look.

He made short work of his appetizer, and she disappeared into the kitchen. She was pleased with his response, he could see. Damn, *he* was pleased. He hadn't eaten anything as interesting and tasty in ages.

Fifteen minutes later she returned with his entrée. He'd poured the wine while she was gone and was taking leisurely sips of a light, peppery Shiraz.

"Okay," she said, setting down his plate in front of him. She hovered for a moment, as though she wanted to fiddle with it some more.

From what he could see, there was nothing more for her to do. The meal was a miniature work of art. Three towers of lamb were arranged in a line. A fourth tower sat alongside them, made up of something very dark, almost black. Sitting in a separate ramekin was something rich and creamy-looking, dusted with cracked pepper.

"It's lamb," she explained. "And...other stuff."

A magical mystery meal. Lifting his glass, he proposed a toast.

"To the chef," he said.

"You might want to eat first before you say that," she said, eyeing the food anxiously.

For the first time he realized she was nervous. This meant a lot to her, he suddenly understood.

"Sophie…"

"Eat!" she said, waving a hand at him. "Put me out of my misery."

Slicing into the lamb, Lucas took a bite. "Mmm. Good. You rolled it in something. Goat cheese?"

"Yes."

On his next pass, he took a slice of the black stuff to accompany his lamb. "My God, what is this?" he asked, registering the salty, tart coldness in his mouth.

"Black olive sorbet," she said.

He laughed. "Wow. Great. It's perfect with the lamb."

She looked hugely relieved. "I liked it, but I wasn't sure…" she said.

"Sophie, it's all amazing. Explain this other thing in the little cup to me."

By the time he'd cleaned his plate, he'd been utterly entertained and entranced. The combination of flavors, temperatures and textures had been inspired.

"Best meal I've had in years," he said with emphasis as he set his cutlery down.

"There's dessert yet," she warned him.

"Bring it on, baby," he said.

But when she came to clear his plate, he pulled her into his lap and kissed her soundly.

"You were worried," he said. "You shouldn't have been. I think you're incredible."

He kissed her again, his fingers sliding into her hair, his tongue dancing with hers.

"It was all a little crazy. I just started putting flavors

together. I think…I think this has all been in the back of my mind for a while. I experimented with a few ideas like this for Sorrentino's, but I chickened out on adding them to the menu."

"Why? People would line up around the block for a meal like this. It's interesting. It's entertaining. It's cheeky and clever."

She blushed and pulled him into a tight, fierce hug. "I'm glad you liked it."

She was blinking away tears when she pulled back, and he caught her chin with his thumb and forefinger and forced her to look him in the eye.

"What's going on?"

She shook her head. "You don't want to hear all my baggage," she said.

He locked his arms tighter around her. "Yeah, I do. You just stuffed me full of food. I won't be ready for dessert for at least an hour. Hit me with it."

A small part of him did a double take at what he'd just heard himself say. Lucas Grant actually encouraging a woman to talk to him about her feelings? Any second now, a litter of pigs was going to fly past the window.

But then Sophie started talking. She told him about her sister, Carrie, and the stunts they used to pull when they were younger, the trouble they'd gotten into. And she told him about the night her sister took the family car for an illicit joyride with her boyfriend, about the accident and the funeral. How hard it had been to sleep alone in the bedroom she'd once shared with her sister.

"I didn't realize it until recently, but Carrie dying really scared me," Sophie said. "It changed me. I'm not sure how it started. I think maybe I wanted to be good for Mom and Dad, because they were so sad afterward. But also…I think I'd seen what had happened to Carrie with all her wildness. It terrified me that I might end up the same way. So, I started playing it safe.

"I chose Brandon because he was safe, and I chose to cook in his family's restaurant because it was safe. And for the past fifteen years I've been toeing the line like a good little girl. Until Brandon pulled the pin. He knew, you see. He knew we were together for the wrong reasons."

She played absently with the neckline of his T-shirt while she spoke, her eyes distant as she tried to articulate her feelings.

"I guess that's why I wanted to cook for you tonight. I wanted to say thank you for helping remind me that life is about risk."

"Me?" he asked, surprised. "What did I do?"

"You walked in the door," she said with a laugh. But he had the feeling she might have said something else if he'd pushed.

He didn't.

She kissed him briefly on the mouth. "Now, dessert."

That night, he tested his bad knee again by reversing their roles for a change. For more than two weeks she'd been on top, and he wanted to be the one giving to her for a change. She clung to him as he slid into her, her legs wrapping around his hips. She was soft and warm and tight and hot and wet and everything good and generous, and he did his utmost to give her the ride of a lifetime.

Afterward, she fell asleep with her arm stretched

across his chest and her face pressed into his shoulder. Brushing a lock of bright hair from her forehead, he closed his eyes and thought about what she'd told him. His last thought before he drifted to sleep was that there were advantages to having no one, belonging nowhere.

THE NIGHT AIR WAS COOL on his skin, and he wove his bike back and forth in a long, wiggly line as he rode through the darkened streets. Houses raced by on either side and he pedaled hard, keen to get to where he was going: home. Home to his place, to where his mom and dad were waiting. No sooner had he thought it than he saw his place up ahead, the familiar solid square of the house looming on his left.

He pressed the brake on his bike, panic surging through him as he got a good look at the house. The front door and all the windows were open and the curtains were streaming out as though someone had turned on a giant fan inside.

Abandoning his bike on the lawn, he took the steps to the porch two at a time. Then he was inside, racing down the hall and into the living room.

He stopped in his tracks, a whimper of fear and confusion rising in his throat as he registered the empty space. Nothing. No carpet, no furniture. Even the light fittings were empty of bulbs. He ran into the kitchen, but it was empty, too. The table and chairs were gone, and the cracked linoleum had been peeled back, leaving only the scarred floorboards. Into the hallway now, flinging doors open as he ran: bathroom, empty. No mirror, no bath. Bedroom, a blank space. Another bedroom. Then a last closed door. Surely they were in there. Surely.

He ran forward, his fingers flattening against the cool wood as he pushed.

The door swung open.

He stared at the empty bed, the only sign that anyone had ever lived in this house, that he'd ever had parents, that he belonged to anyone.

"No!" he cried. "No!"

"Lucas. Lucas!"

The sound of Sophie's concerned voice snapped Lucas back to consciousness, and he became abruptly aware that his body was as taut as a bow. Sophie was leaning over him, her face a pale blur in the dark night.

"Goddamn," he said.

Again. He'd had the nightmare *again*. He thought he'd beaten it. It had been two weeks. What the hell was going on with his head?

He heard the sheets rustle, and then Sophie's bedside lamp flicked on. Without a word she slid from the bed and disappeared into the bathroom. He heard the tap running and she returned with a tall glass of water for him. She handed it over wordlessly, then sat cross-legged on the bed, facing him.

"It was the same dream, wasn't it?" she asked when he'd gulped half the glass of water.

"It's no big deal."

"I disagree. This is the third time you've had it in as many weeks. That I know of, anyway. It wouldn't surprise me if you'd had it more often. There's obviously something on your mind, Lucas."

"Sophie, seriously. It's sweet of you to be concerned about me, but there really is nothing to worry about."

It came out more firmly than he'd intended, and she was silent for a long time, studying him thoughtfully. Then she took a deep breath.

"I know about your parents, Lucas. About the state homes and the foster placements."

She was careful to keep her voice neutral, but he could see the sympathy in her eyes anyway.

That goddamned book.

It was out—and people had noticed. And now everyone was going to look at him the way Sophie was. Every time he did publicity for a movie, every interview he ever gave from now on, they'd always be referencing his goddamned childhood. Asking about his parents, about what had happened. Pushing, wanting to know all the things he'd buried deep down inside.

"How?" he asked, needing confirmation. "When?"

"My friend called me from Sydney this afternoon. She knows I'm working for you, and there was an excerpt from a new biography in the newspaper."

"Jesus Christ."

The daily paper, for Pete's sake.

Why hadn't Derek warned him? He paid the guy hundreds of thousands of dollars every year to take care of this crap, and he'd had no warning…. Suddenly he remembered that Derek had left a message on his cell phone, but he'd yet to return the call. Shit.

"I'm sorry, I thought you must have known about the book," she said, her face creased with concern.

"I did. I was hoping it would crash and burn," he said, dragging a hand through his hair.

She spoke slowly, obviously trying to pick her words

with care. "I know it's an appalling invasion of privacy, but you don't have anything to be ashamed of, Lucas. Your childhood isn't something you need to hide."

"I'm not ashamed of my childhood," he said. It wasn't shame that made him not want to talk about any of it—he simply didn't want it to exist. He'd spent his entire adult life proving to himself that he didn't give a shit that his parents had dumped him like yesterday's garbage.

And now some spineless turd of a journalist had dug up his secrets and the rest of the world wanted to poke him with a stick to see what made him tick.

"Listen, I don't want to talk about this."

"Okay, I understand that," Sophie said. "But what about the nightmares?"

"Sophie…"

"Lucas, there is obviously something you need to deal with here. Something to do with your family, your parents—"

"I don't remember my parents. They dumped me when I was four years old. I know nothing about them, so the dream is not about them," he said tersely.

Sophie simply continued to hold his eye. "Have you ever thought about talking to someone?" she suggested quietly.

Lucas heaved a great, angry, frustrated sigh. "Here we go."

"It might help."

"No, it won't. I get on just fine, in case you hadn't noticed."

She raised her eyebrows at him.

"The nightmares will go away. They always do."

"You've had them before?" She sounded appalled.

"Look. It doesn't matter."

"It does. These things do matter. Like me and Carrie. You need to look it in the eye and deal with it, Lucas."

Suddenly it all clicked into place—the special meal, the cozy chat about her sister. All of it coming on the heels of her little discovery.

"I get it. That's what tonight was all about, right? You offering up your sad little story of family suffering so poor old Lucas would spill his guts about his. You know what? I don't need your pity and I certainly don't need your amateur attempts at psychology. You think you know me, just because we screwed a few times…"

He shook his head and spread his hands in the air to indicate how little it all meant, how far off the mark she was.

Her jaw worked, and she blinked a few times. Then she rolled to the edge of the bed.

She waited until she'd hauled on a T-shirt and a pair of shorts before speaking.

"You're an asshole."

Then she walked.

He'd wanted to hurt her. To make her back off, to stop pushing.

He'd succeeded.

SOPHIE FOUGHT TEARS as she made her way to the cottage.

Angry tears, she assured herself, *because I want to punch him, but I can't. He probably has his face insured for a bazillion dollars and I'd wind up getting sued.*

The cottage had an abandoned air when she let

herself in the front door and turned on a light. Somehow, she ended up in Lucas's bed every night, and gradually almost all of her clothes had migrated to his suite in the main house. Now, the only things left to show she'd ever moved into the cottage were some stray personal items scattered about.

She paced the living room, trying to work off some of her anger. She was not his whipping boy. And she wasn't going to feel wrong or guilty for caring about him, for trying to help him heal. She'd tried to help. Big freakin' crime.

The worst thing was, she knew he didn't mean it. She knew that he liked her, that he cared for her. They'd become friends, at the very least. Intimate friends. But she'd gotten too close and she'd pushed him and he'd punished her. Because he was so screwed up about his childhood. About his parents— she was absolutely positive on that front now. His problems had something to do with them. Even though he said he couldn't remember anything, his dream and his reaction tonight told her everything she needed to know.

She looked up as the front door banged open. Lucas waited until he was standing in front of her before he spoke.

"That was a shitty thing to say. I shouldn't have taken my temper out on you," he said quietly.

"Yep," she said.

"And you're right, I am an asshole."

"Uh-huh."

"And you're more than just a screw to me."

She shrugged a shoulder, even though she was inordinately pleased to hear him say it out loud.

"If I do the dishes for a week and give you a foot massage every day, will you forgive me?" he asked. He flashed her his movie-star smile.

"We have a dishwasher," she said, refusing to be charmed. Oh, but she'd forgotten how compelling he could be when he put his mind to it.

"I'll let you be on top," he said next, moving closer.

She held her ground, and his chest brushed the tips of her breasts.

"I'll let you win at Scrabble."

She scoffed, "Let me win. You've beaten me once, pal. *Once.*"

He smiled at her then, sliding a hand around the back of her neck and capturing her nape in the palm of his hand. He kissed her, a long, slow, thorough kiss that only ended when he rested his cheek against hers and spoke quietly into her ear.

"I'm sorry, Sophie. You deserve better. Forgive me?" he asked.

His voice was low and husky and infinitely sincere. She smoothed his hair back from his forehead.

"Of course." Of course she forgave him. She probably always would, damn his eyes.

12

PERPHAPS IT WAS HER imagination, but Sophie felt as though the dynamic shifted between them after that night. There was something more in Lucas's eyes when he looked at her, and certainly she felt a definite lurch in the general region of her heart when she looked at him. Their friendship had deepened. They'd acknowledged their mutual unwillingness to hurt each other.

They valued each other.

She woke on the last morning of their third week together with the thought fully formed in her mind. As usual, Lucas was still sleeping beside her, and she rolled onto her side to watch him. He had ridiculously long eyelashes for a man, and when he slept they brushed his cheeks. With his guard down, she could imagine him as the boy he once was, and she felt a tug of sadness and regret for the difficult path he'd had in life. He'd made so much of himself, and he'd come from such a hard place. He had a lot to be proud of, but she knew he didn't see it that way.

Not that they'd talked about the book again, or his dreams. And he hadn't had another nightmare, although she suspected the two stiff whiskeys he'd taken to drinking before bedtime had something to do with that.

Unfortunately, the rest of the world could not be blocked out so readily. She knew from conversations—arguments—she'd overheard him having with Derek that he'd had interview requests resulting from the biography. The moment he returned to Sydney, he would be inundated with media. And she had no idea how he was going to deal with any of it.

But, of course, as he'd made quite clear, that wasn't any of her business.

Unable to resist touching him, Sophie traced the curve of his ear. They had one week left together. The thought made her stomach muscles tense with anticipated loss. It was going to be hard to walk away from him, from their time together. But she was under no illusions—their time together *would* end. She hadn't become that foolish, at least. Hadn't taken that last, perilous step toward inevitable pain.

In the meantime, they had seven whole days to spend with each other, and she planned to relish every minute of every hour.

Accordingly, she woke Lucas in the nicest possible way and they had drowsy morning sex, slow and sultry. Then she cooked them both breakfast, and afterward they lay on the couch doing a crossword puzzle with the morning sun streaming across their bodies.

She lay lengthwise with her bare feet in his lap, and he rubbed her arches absently with his free hand as he contemplated the folded newspaper.

"Twenty-five down. We're looking for an African animal in five letters," he said. "You'd think they could be more specific. That's a big continent we're talking about there."

"Try hyena," she suggested. "Or tiger."

"Tigers are from India," he said.

"Really? Oh, yeah. Of course," she said.

He flashed her a smile and rubbed her arch again. "Hyena fits, though."

"See? There is method in my madness," she said.

He was about to read out the next clue when his cell rang. He scowled.

"If that's Derek calling me to hassle about those scripts again…" he muttered as he reached to grab his phone off the coffee table.

Sophie watched his face as he took the call, trying to sort out his relationship with the much-maligned Derek. It hadn't escaped her notice that Lucas seemed to disagree with his manager on a whole host of subjects—how much press he should be doing, what kind of movies Lucas should be making and all the St. Barnaby's stuff being at the top of the list. Perhaps, she mused, they had one of those jostling male relationships, like Tom Cruise and Cuba Gooding Jr. in *Jerry McGuire*.

"Adele. How the hell are you?" Lucas asked, the scowl on his face turning into a smile.

Not wanting to eavesdrop, Sophie started to stand so as to give him privacy to take his call, but Lucas's grip tightened on her feet and he shook his head at her, indicating the call would only take a minute. She settled back onto the cushions and reached for the crossword puzzle.

Deliberately tuning out his conversation, she'd filled

in the top right-hand corner of the puzzle before she heard something that made her stiffen.

"Tomorrow night? God, I'd forgotten. Of course I'll be there. I wouldn't miss it for anything," he said. "What time do you want me?"

Sophie felt an absurd lurch of dismay. Lucas was going to leave.

God. It was over. She'd thought they had another week, but he was about to pull out now and, somehow, she had to find the strength to shrug it off and act as though it didn't matter.

Carefully she schooled her face into what she hoped was a carefree expression as he wound up the call. It took all her strength of will to glance at him casually when he finally put the phone down.

"We're looking for a vegetable with six letters," she said.

But he was looking apologetic, and she knew the time for cozy crossword puzzles was over. A tight feeling banded her chest and she let the paper drop into her lap.

Here it is, the big goodbye, she thought.

"Soph, that was an old friend of mine from drama-school days," he said. "She's an artist now, and her latest exhibition opens tomorrow night in Sydney. Unfortunately, I promised her months ago that I'd be there."

"Sure," Sophie said with a shrug. "I understand. You have to head back a little early."

She started moving her feet off his lap again, but Lucas frowned and wouldn't let go of her ankles.

"No. I'll go back for just the one night—it's only

an hour or so by car. And I want you to come with me," he said.

She stared at him, aware that a dangerous relief was surging through her veins. "Really?" Her voice was high with relieved incredulity, and she gave herself a mental slap. *Dignity, girl. Have a little dignity.*

"Of course. I'm not going to leave you here on your own. And I'm not giving up the rest of my time off, either."

"I'll have to stop by my apartment to grab something to wear," she said, thinking of her good pair of black heels and her all-purpose little black dress.

"We'll make a day of it, and I'll take you shopping," he said.

She narrowed her eyes at him. "You're *not* buying me a dress, Lucas," she said repressively, although a little part of her quite liked the idea. Too many viewings of *Pretty Woman,* obviously.

"Fine. But I still want to take you shopping," he said. "Donatella says I have a good eye."

She stared at him, pretty sure that the Donatella he was talking about usually came accessorized with a Versace after her name. Every now and then she forgot who he was and what he did. He'd become so human to her, so normal and flawed like everyone else in the world.

"I'm not wearing anything with safety pins holding it together," she warned him.

"We'll see."

He snatched the crossword puzzle back, giving her a dark look when he saw how much she'd done without him.

"What can I say? I have a good vocabulary," she said.

"You have a dirty vocabulary," he corrected her.

He bent his head to the page, and she studied him covertly from beneath her lashes. She was going to Sydney with Lucas. They were going to a flashy event, and she was going to be his date. More importantly, they were taking their relationship beyond the confines of this house and the Blue Mountains. After their single foray into the nearby mountain town of Faulconbridge that first week, they'd stuck to the estate. They had everything they needed shipped in—food arrived on a weekly basis, and a discreet, virtually invisible cleaner whisked through the house magically every other day. There was no need for anything else, since they'd been so wrapped up in enjoying each other.

Now the bubble was about to burst. Not quite permanently—not yet. But soon, it would all be over.

Probably that was a good thing, given how dismayed she'd felt when she'd heard Lucas committing to attending Adele's opening. The wash of regret and hurt that had swept over her had been far stronger than anything she'd anticipated. Maybe she was a lot more foolish that she had been prepared to admit to herself, after all. Maybe—

"Idiot," she muttered under her breath, and Lucas glanced up from the crossword. He cocked an eyebrow at her in query, and she waved a hand back toward the newspaper.

"Come on, what's the next clue?" she asked.

It was too late to pull out now. The damage was already done. She might as well enjoy her time left in the sun.

Lucas pressed the accelerator to the floor and shifted down a gear. Beside him, Sophie turned her face into the wind, her short, bright hair a ruffled mess, her face all but swallowed up by her Jackie O sunglasses.

"You look like a mad squirrel in those sunglasses," he said.

"Funny, I was just thinking that you look like a racing ferret in yours," she said, eyeing his sleek, modern frames disparagingly. He laughed, and realized that he hadn't looked forward to a public event as much in a long time. Usually he turned up, smiled, chatted to whoever was important or beautiful, then got the hell out as quickly as possible—usually to find somewhere noisier where people were wearing less clothing and drinking stronger drinks.

"I forgot to say, Derek's made an appointment for me at the hospital this afternoon," he said. "They want to check on everything."

Sophie looked at him, a worried frown appearing between her eyebrows.

"You haven't exactly been resting your knee," she said, clearly thinking of some of their more recent bedroom activities. "I hope it's all right."

"It'll be fine, don't worry," he said, amused by her concern. "All that exercise has been good for it, I'm sure."

They bantered and teased one another the rest of the way into the city, and nearly a full hour and a half after their departure they were pulling up outside his Double Bay harborside home.

"Every time I catch a ferry across the harbor I look at these houses and wonder who is lucky enough to live here," she said as he drove his car through the automatic garage door.

"Now you know," he said. "Nicole Kidman is around the point a bit. And Russell Crowe has a pad on the end of the Woolloomooloo pier."

"Cozy. I suppose you have Trivial Pursuit nights and whatnot?" she asked, poker-faced.

"All the time. And key-swapping parties."

She gave him a dry look at that.

"What? It's true, I swear. Keith Urban is a tiger in the sack," he said.

She punched him for that one, and he ruffled her hair in retaliation. That led to a heated, heavy petting session in the dark quiet of his garage. He had her in his lap and his hands under her tank top when someone cleared his throat loudly.

Sophie stiffened and blushed furiously as the overhead light came on.

"Lucas. Great to see you," Derek said, but his eyes were on Sophie as she slithered from Lucas's lap to her own side of the car, furtively rearranging her clothes all the while.

Lucas frowned. As usual, Derek's timing sucked large.

"Derek," he said.

"I don't think we've met before," Derek said pointedly to Sophie.

It was Derek's business to mind Lucas's business, but he bristled at the speculation in the other man's gaze.

"This is Sophie," he said. Derek didn't need to know any more than that. Certainly he didn't need to know that Sophie was the chef that Julie Jenkins had hired.

Somehow he knew Derek would find that piece of information highly amusing.

"Hi," Sophie said, looking up properly for the first time and giving a tight, embarrassed little wave.

Derek frowned, and Lucas knew exactly what he was thinking, the same thing that he'd thought when he first met Sophie: that she was nothing special.

How wrong could one man be? Thank God he'd had a chance to look twice, past the expectations created by too many years surrounded by silicone, BOTOX and the latest fad workout.

"Come on, Soph. I'll show you around," he said, getting out of the car and pulling his crutches from the space behind the driver's seat.

"I've got some papers for you to sign," Derek said, falling in behind them as they entered the house. "And Steven Spielberg wants to do a phone conference on the Scott Frank script at eleven."

"No can do. I'm taking Sophie shopping," Lucas said as he led Sophie into the living room.

He watched as she took in the stark white walls, modern art and sleek leather furniture. She glanced into the next room, spotting the vast glass-topped dining table, more white walls and more modern art. She didn't say a word, or frown, or even purse her lips. Still, he knew she hated it. And, looking at it all with new eyes, he could see why a warm, vibrant person like Sophie might find his house a little…sterile. Maybe even cold and unwelcoming.

Derek was making impatient noises behind them, and Lucas swung around to face him.

"Look, I'm still on a break until next week. You

shouldn't have made any commitments without asking me first. Just tell Steven I'll call him next week. He'll be cool."

"I can go shopping on my own. I don't mind," Sophie said, looking back and forth between the two of them.

"See? Sophie's fine with it," Derek said.

"But I'm not. Reschedule," Lucas said. He wasn't about to dump Sophie like a hot potato because Hollywood beckoned.

Derek shot Sophie a frustrated look as he headed for the door. "Fine. I'll see you this afternoon at the hospital," he said.

Sophie pulled a face once they heard the front door close.

"He's not happy," she said.

"Tough. He'll own me again next week. This week is mine," he said.

Reaching for her, he pulled her close. "You hate my house, don't you?" he asked as he nuzzled her neck.

"Why do you say that?" she said. As a stalling tactic it was masterful, but he was on to her.

"I can tell." He nipped at her earlobe.

"The view is fantastic. Awesome," she said, her hands curving into his butt to pull him closer.

"Very diplomatic."

"Do *you* like it?" she asked. "Surely that's the most important thing."

Lucas lifted his face from her neck and glanced around again. "Not really. But I guess I don't spend enough time here to care."

"So you're based mostly in L.A., then?" she asked.

"I'm based wherever the next film is being shot. Actor's curse." He shrugged.

Her eyes were solemn as she looked at him. "That must get lonely. Never having a place that's all your own."

He could see what she was thinking, the connections she was making, and he pulled away from her.

"I'll show you the bedroom," he said, leering at her comically. "Then we can hit the shops."

She eyed him seriously for a long beat before nodding. "It's your show, lead on."

13

SHOPPING BAGS IN HAND, Sophie let herself into her apartment later that afternoon. Lucas had dropped her off before heading over to the hospital, promising to collect her later for dinner before the gallery opening.

The apartment was stuffy after so many weeks of being shut up, and she opened windows and doors before moving into the bedroom and dropping her shopping bags onto the bed. It was strange to be home. Looking around the bedroom she used to share with Brandon, she felt as though she was looking at another person's life. For three weeks, she'd been living in the lap of luxury with one of the world's most charismatic men. But *this* was her life—this apartment, her day-to-day existence as a chef, her tight-knit circle of family and friends. It was probably timely for her to remember that since she'd just spent a sinful amount of money on a dress that Lucas had helped her choose. Sophie Gallagher was an off-the-rack girl, not a designer original. Today, the past few weeks were the exception, not the rule.

She was putting the kettle on to make coffee when she heard a key in the door and Brandon appeared in the kitchen. He stopped dead in his tracks when he saw her.

"Sophie."

"Brandon."

"I've been collecting the mail," he said, displaying a handful of envelopes.

"Oh. Okay, thanks," she said. It was strange seeing him again. Her whole world had changed since they last saw each other.

"You're very tanned," Brandon said.

"I guess." Sophie held out an arm and considered it. She *was* brown. She had no tan lines, either, thanks to all the skinny-dipping she and Lucas had been indulging in.

"So, how is the job?" Brandon asked. "We've missed you at the restaurant."

"I've missed you guys, too," Sophie said, although she felt a little like a fraud. She'd been so immersed in Lucas and her new recipes, she really hadn't thought about much from her old life.

"Monty's been doing a good job as head chef, but I think he'll be pretty happy to see you back," Brandon said. There was a question in his tone and the look he shot her.

She took a deep breath. "I won't be coming back, Brandon."

Brandon's shoulders sagged. "I suspected you'd say that. Mom and Dad will be disappointed. But to be honest, I'm happy for you," he said.

She must have looked as surprised as she felt, because he quickly explained himself.

"You were always better than us, Soph. We were lucky to keep you for as long as we did. You wait— you're going to make a big splash somewhere."

She blinked. "Thanks," she finally said.

The kettle had well and truly boiled, and she automatically grabbed two coffee mugs.

"You'll stay?" she asked.

He nodded. Then all of a sudden she realized she *had* missed him, even if she hadn't been conscious of it. He'd been her friend and lover for nearly half her life, and there would always be a place for him in her heart. She'd been angry with him for pulling the rug out from beneath her, but he'd done the right thing. For both of them.

They sat at the kitchen table and talked, Brandon filling her in on restaurant scuttlebutt, catching her up on family stuff. It was nice. Comfortable. She could almost understand why she'd taken refuge in it for so long. But in no way was she tempted to go back.

Finally he stood to leave.

"You look great, Soph. Happy," he said. He seemed worried for her, and because it felt right, Sophie stepped forward and put her arms around him.

"Yes," she said. They held each other long and tight. "Thank you for having the courage to do what I couldn't," she whispered. "It's been scary, but you were right."

He squeezed her one last time, and when he pulled back from her she saw his eyes were filled with tears.

"I'll always love you, Soph," he said.

"You, too."

They smiled at each other, then he left.

Sophie stood in the middle of their apartment for a few beats, marveling at how far her feelings had shifted in the space of only a few weeks.

Then she shook off her moment of introspection.

Lucas would be there in an hour, and she had a lot of work to do if she was going to be rubbing shoulders with Sydney's elite.

LUCAS TOOK THE STEPS to Sophie's apartment two at a time, just because he could. The doctor and the physiotherapist had been so pleased with his ultrasound and his range of movement that they'd both agreed the braces and crutches could go. He still had to be careful while his tendons continued to heal, but it was like being let out of prison. He wanted to dance, run, climb and kick up his heels all at once. And he wanted to do it all with Sophie.

Rapping on the shiny red door to her apartment, he glanced at his watch. They had a dinner reservation at six, then they were going on to the gallery. Maybe later they could sneak out the back way and find someplace to dance all night.

All thought was suspended when Sophie opened the door. She was wearing her new dress, and his mouth went dry with pure lust.

"Wow," he said.

Made from a mocha-brown silk, her dress sat just off her shoulders, baring the skin of her neck and chest and showcasing her breasts. The waist was nipped in with a thick band, and the skirt flared out to end in a kicky row of ruffles at her knees. He'd seen her in it when she tried it on in the boutique and it had looked pretty great then. But now she'd made her eyes up with some kind of golden-green eye shadow, and her lips glistened wickedly with gloss. She looked hot.

"You're walking!" she said, her eyes widening.

"You're gorgeous," he said, hands already reaching for her.

She blushed and smoothed a hand down the skirt of the dress. "I'll probably fall over and break my leg in these crazy shoes." She extended a foot to display one of the dark-chocolate stilettos he'd chosen for her that afternoon.

"If you fall, I promise to catch you," he said, sliding his hands around her back and down onto her silk-covered butt. He frowned when he registered there was nothing but a single layer of silk beneath his hands.

"Ms. Gallagher, are you commando beneath all those frills?"

"It's a thong. This fabric is a bitch for panty lines."

He was already hard, but he grew harder still at the thought of Sophie wearing a thong and four-inch stilettos.

"Show me," he demanded.

"Don't we have reservations for dinner?" she asked.

"Show me," he repeated.

The look she shot him was pure minx as she stepped away from him. Sliding her hands down the fabric of her skirt, she found the ruffled hem and slowly lifted it to reveal her bare, tanned thighs and a delicate triangle of cinnamon-colored lace.

"Turn around," he growled, his hands curling in anticipation.

She swiveled on one heel, tossing a coy glance over her shoulder as she flipped up the back of her skirt so he could see her butt framed by twin curves of lace.

His breath hissed out between his teeth. "Do you have any idea how hot you look right now?" he said.

Her skirt still gathered around her waist, she cocked a knee forward, pushing her butt out more. "You like?" she asked.

Since he'd always believed that actions spoke louder than words, he closed the distance between them, his hands cupping her bare cheeks reverently.

"I like a lot," he said.

She was standing a few feet away from the wall, and she reached out and braced her hands against it, pushing into his hands more firmly. He groaned and slid his fingers along the line of her thong until he was delving into the steamy heat between her thighs. She was wet for him already, and he traced a finger over the heart of her, pressing through the delicate lace of her thong. She circled her hips, silently encouraging his exploration, and he slid a finger beneath the lace and into her.

"*Yessss,*" she murmured, leaning forward more to deepen the angle of his penetration.

He slid his other hand around her hip and down over her belly, cupping her mound with his palm as his middle finger found her clit.

"Lucas," she moaned, and he knew exactly what she wanted. Breaking contact with her for a beat, he unzipped his fly. She widened her stance, her butt arching high, and he slid her thong to one side as he nudged her slick inner lips with his hardness. Holding his breath, savoring the moment, he slid into her, clenching his hands on her hips as he registered how right and sweet she felt.

"You feel so damn good," he murmured as he slowly withdrew almost to the point of no return before once again sliding inside her to the hilt.

"So do you," she panted. "You feel amazing."

Hands running up the backs of her thighs now, he worked her slowly, lingering over each thrust, each wave of sensation. He could feel her whole body quivering beneath his hands as the urgency built, driving him from slow and sensual to hard and demanding. He snaked a hand over her hip again and underneath her thong. Her clitoris was swollen with need and he slicked his fingers over and over her as he plunged again and again.

Her hands fisted against the wall and he felt her knees buckle as they found their peak together. He ground into her, his grip on her waist keeping her upright as he lost it.

They were both out of breath, and he pressed a kiss onto her shoulder as he withdrew from her. He felt the loss of her warmth, and her high heels clicked on the wood floor as she straightened.

"Note to self, wear lace underwear more often," she said as she turned around to face him.

Her eyes were cloudy with passion, and he reached out to rub a thumb along her cheekbone. Right now, she was the most beautiful woman he'd ever seen.

She caught sight of his watch as he withdrew his hand, and she gasped.

"We are *so* late," she said. "In fact, they've probably given our table away."

"Who cares?" he said. "Who says we even need to go to that stupid opening anyway?"

She swatted his hand away when he tried to see down the neckline of her dress.

"Your friend is expecting you," she said.

Another great thing about Sophie—her loyalty. He'd

bet she was the one person a friend could always rely on, no matter what.

"I know. We'll go to Harry's Café de Wheels," she said.

"God, I haven't been there for years," he said, flashing back to his old drama-school years.

"Come on."

They found a park right out the front of the Woolloomooloo wharves and stood in line to place their orders at the window of the brightly painted pie cart that had become a Sydney institution after nearly seventy years of operation.

"S'good," Sophie murmured around a mouthful of buttery pastry, and Lucas repressed the impulse to ruffle her hair affectionately. Just twenty minutes ago she'd been driving him wild with her earthy sensuality, but now she looked like a well-dressed urchin, with a paper napkin tucked into the neckline of her dress to prevent disasters as she ate a hot meat pie with lots of tomato sauce.

"Don't tell Derek I fed you a meat pie," she said. "He'll sack me for making his meal ticket blimp out."

"What Derek doesn't know won't hurt him," he said. He frowned as he remembered the conversation he'd had with Derek while they'd waited for the doctor this afternoon.

"Be careful with that one," Derek had said, from which Lucas had assumed he meant Sophie.

He'd remained silent, not wanting to discuss her with Derek, but it hadn't stopped his manager from wading in.

"I mean it, Lucas. She's not one of your usual women. You make sure she knows the score when you walk away. I don't want to have to handle her, and the last thing we want is some tell-all in the tabloids."

Derek's comment had made Lucas see red. He'd rounded on his manager before he could stop himself.

"Don't talk about her ever again, okay? She's not someone you are ever going to have to *handle*."

Derek had taken a step backward and held up his hands as though Lucas had pulled a gun on him.

"Chill, man. I'm just doing my job," he'd said.

But neither of them had mentioned her name again.

Now, Lucas wrapped his arm around her waist as they walked back to his car. Suddenly she stopped in her tracks.

"God I just realized—are there going to be reporters there?" she asked uncertainly.

"Yes. That's kind of the whole point of me going. Adele wants the publicity."

Sophie bit her lip. He reached across and caught her hand.

"I've already got it covered, don't worry. We'll go in separately. That way they won't know we're together," he suggested. "You won't have to deal with them."

"I was thinking about you. About…you know," she said.

Running the gauntlet of the paparazzi could be daunting at the best of times, and it would be a totally new experience for Sophie. But she wasn't nervous for herself—she was worried about him, because she knew he bitterly resented what the biography had done to his private life.

"Tonight will just be photographers," he assured her. "No one knows I'm coming."

"Okay. Good."

She was looking relieved. For him.

For the first time he had an inkling of just how lucky he'd gotten when Julie Jenkins approached Sophie to be his private chef. She was one in a million.

And in another week's time, he was going to let her go, the way he always let his women go—easy, with a smile.

Which probably made him the world's biggest fool.

14

WATCHING LUCAS ARRIVE at the opening made Sophie feel like Alice through the looking glass.

Standing to one side near the entrance of the gallery, watching the flashes pop and the photographers jostle for position, she experienced a surreal sense of vertigo. Had she really slept with the stunningly gorgeous man climbing out of the Porsche and onto the red carpet? Had she really threaded her fingers through his dark hair and caressed his tall, hard body?

It simply didn't seem possible when he was standing here, the center of everything.

Unable to look away, she followed his progress along the red carpet and into the gallery as avidly and hungrily as everyone else. When he was gone, it felt as though the night grew a little darker, the air a little colder.

Wrapping her arms around herself, she considered her enormous folly in thinking she could dally with this man for a few weeks and walk away unscathed. Had she been *insane?* The man was a walking, talking god. Of course she was going to become infatuated with him. It had been inevitable.

"Idiot," she said under her breath. She'd been saying

that to herself a bit lately, she'd noticed. Probably because she'd been behaving like an idiot.

"Lucas asked me to come out and escort you in."

Sophie swung around to see Derek standing there, looking none too pleased with his babysitting duty. She felt the weight of his gaze as it dropped to her breasts, and embarrassed heat rush up into her face as she remembered how he'd found her with Lucas's hands up her top in the garage this morning.

"Nice dress," he said as she fell in alongside him.

She knew exactly what he was thinking: that Lucas had bought it for her. She felt the need to correct him, but she stopped herself. Derek had nothing to do with her and Lucas.

"Before we go in…" Derek said, halting just inside the doorway. "I hope you're not taking Lucas too seriously, Sophie. Don't expect him to hang around, or call you after a few weeks to ask you to fly out to join him on set or something crazy. He doesn't work like that. He doesn't do relationships. Okay?"

Sophie eyed him steadily but didn't say a word.

"I mean it. Don't think you're in line for a wedding ring or something ridiculous," Derek said, frowning at her nonreaction. "Lucas has a lot of women in his life. A lot. And, not to put too fine a point on it, some of them are real stunners. Just a word from the wise."

She wasn't quite sure where her calm came from; perhaps from her outrage that this man had taken it upon himself to warn her off so dismissively. He'd managed to call her deluded, unattractive and disposable in the space of a few seconds. What a gem.

"Are you finished?" she asked.

Derek shut his jaw with a click and Sophie shouldered her way through the crowd.

She should have taken Derek's little pep talk as a sign that her evening was about to take a turn for the worse. Inside, the gallery was full of beautiful people, all of them glittering and tall and slim. Instantly her very expensive dress became very average, and she felt painfully aware of her every flaw—too short, too curvy, too redheaded.

This is why I don't read fashion magazines, she told herself as she stared at a rail-thin, painfully gorgeous woman that she recognized as a top international model. It was simply not possible for her to stand in the same room with so much perfection and retain a grip on her own self-esteem.

Switching her attention from the people to the artwork, Sophie's heart sank further. More brutal, bright modern art—lots of blobby paint, smears and asymmetrical patterns. Not her cup of tea—but then, she was hardly the market she realized when she saw a price list lying abandoned on a nearby table.

"Sophie," Lucas said, and she turned to find him bearing down on her, two champagne glasses in hand. After he'd handed one over, his fingers closed around her elbow. "Where were you? I was worried."

Instantly she was warmed by his attention. "Sorry. I was a little freaked out. It's pretty crazy out there."

He smiled sympathetically and squeezed her elbow reassuringly. "Have some champagne and you'll feel better."

She followed his advice, but it didn't make much difference, especially when Adele—another beautiful person—sailed over and grabbed Lucas, dragging him off to meet someone. To his credit, Lucas came straight back to her, and the next time Adele drew him away he towed Sophie with him. But no one was interested in talking to her. After Lucas introduced her, they inevitably gave her a polite smile and a quick head-to-toe before turning all their focus on him. Plus, she knew nothing about art. Nothing, nada, zilch. And since all the conversation was about Adele's work and how it "talked to the schism at the center of the disjuncted self," she was reduced to nodding occasionally and shifting from foot to foot to ease her aching toes.

After an hour she told Lucas she was going to the bathroom and slipped off into the crowd. It took her a good ten minutes to find someone who looked unglamorous enough to be staff so she could ask where the ladies' was, and when she came back to Lucas he was surrounded by a group of laughing men and women. She recognized a politician, a television star and an up-and-coming singer among them. Rather than elbow her way back to his side, she found an inconspicuous space along the wall and leaned against it, taking turns easing first one foot and then the other out of the torture of her shoes.

If only Adele hadn't followed up with Lucas's invitation, we'd still be holed up in our own private little world in the Blue Mountains, she thought wistfully. She grimaced at the childishness of her own thoughts. Maybe Derek had been right to warn her off, after all.

"Come on, we're going."

Sophie glanced up from studying the squashed and

maimed toes of her left foot to find Lucas standing in front of her.

"Sorry?" she asked stupidly, sliding her foot back into her shoe and straightening.

"We're getting out of here," he said.

"What about Adele?" she asked, even as her heart soared with relief.

"I've done my bit. She's got her publicity. Come on."

One arm around her waist, he steered her through the crowd toward the doorway the caterers had been swinging in and out of all night.

Weaving past the catering staff, they exited the kitchen door and found themselves in the alleyway behind the gallery.

"This way," Lucas said, tugging her to the right.

She tried to keep up with him, but her killer heels had reduced her to hobbling by now and Lucas finally registered her discomfort.

"What's wrong?" he asked.

"Blisters. And I think all my toes are dislocated," Sophie said, eyeing the pointy toes on the stilettos ruefully.

Lucas looked guilty. "That's probably my fault. You warned me you don't usually wear heels."

"They're beautiful shoes," she said diplomatically. "And I wanted them very badly."

Presenting her with his back, Lucas looked at her over his shoulder. "Hop on."

She stared at him.

"Come on, hop on, or it'll be three in the morning by the time we make it back to the mountains."

"We're going back tonight?" she asked, surprised.

The original plan had been for them to stay the night in Sydney and drive back to the Jenkinses' estate the next day.

"You don't really want to stay in the sensory deprivation tank, do you?"

He was referring to his white-on-white apartment, and since he'd already guessed her feelings, she was free to be honest.

"Not really."

"Then giddyap."

Shaking her head at his silliness, she looped her hands around his neck and hoisted herself onto his back. His hands hooked beneath her knees and he started up the alleyway with a firm, confident step.

"I'm not too heavy?" she asked. He *had* just come. off crutches, after all.

"Sophie, you're practically a midget," he reminded her.

Leaning forward, she inhaled his aftershave and pressed her cheek next to his.

"I could get used to this," she said. In truth, she was touched by his consideration. He'd cut out of the opening early, and now he was driving her back to the estate because he wanted her to be happy and comfortable. Out of nowhere, tears pricked at the backs of her eyes and she tightened her grip around his chest, hugging him to her.

"Everything okay back there?" he asked as they neared the main road where his car was parked.

"Sure," she said, blinking the silly tears away.

"Let me just check to see if there are any photographers still lurking," he said. "Usually they bugger off after everyone has arrived."

Attempting to keep a low profile, he ducked his head around the corner.

"Looks like the coast is clear."

Sophie burst into giggles.

"What's so funny?"

"Kind of hard to be subtle with me on your back," she said, imagining how ridiculous they must look.

They were both still laughing as they approached his car and a large bus whizzed past in the narrow street, generating a strong gust of wind in its wake. Startled, Sophie felt the back of her skirt fly up, and she had a sudden mental image of her lace-thonged butt being displayed to the world as she rode piggyback on Lucas Grant's back. Whooping with alarm, she pressed a frantic hand behind herself, desperately trying to hold her skirt down while laughing at the same time over how insanely foolish she must look. The flash of a camera caught them both by surprise. His grin fading abruptly, Lucas let her slide to the ground as he turned to face the lurking paparazzo.

"Who are you with?" he asked, his handsome face dark and uncompromising as he approached the guy.

The photographer lay his hand protectively over his camera. *"The Daily Telegraph,"* he said.

"I'll give you five thousand for the picture," he said.

Sophie nearly choked. Was he kidding?

"Do you know what this is worth on the international market? U.S. rights alone…?" the photographer said.

"Fine. Tell me what you want, my manager will make sure you get it," Lucas said.

Sophie could see the tension in his body and she stepped forward. "Lucas, it's okay."

"No, it's not. You're not up for grabs. You didn't choose this."

"One picture of you giving me a piggyback is not worth tens of thousands of dollars," she said.

"Hundreds of thousands," the photographer interjected helpfully. "Plus there's the photo credit."

Lucas had been focusing on her, but now his gaze swiveled around and fixed once again on the paparazzo.

"How much?"

"Lucas," Sophie insisted.

His gaze was dark with anger when he glanced at her. "Sophie, stay out of it."

"Sophie. Nice name," the photographer said, and she realized they'd just given him a caption.

"How much?"

But the paparazzo just smiled and shook his head. "It's not for sale. Sorry. I'll be able to pay my mortgage off with this baby."

A muscle clenched in Lucas's jaw and he took a menacing step forward. Sophie scrambled to place herself between him and the suddenly nervous photographer.

"Lucas. Look at me," she said, staring at his face until he met her eye. "Forget it. I don't care. Okay?"

His gaze remained dark and troubled for a beat, but then it cleared.

"Let's go home," she said quietly, placing a hand on his chest.

"Home. Right. Where's that?" the photographer asked hopefully.

Sophie swung around so sharply that he took a step backward.

"Don't push your luck, buddy," she said.

When she turned back, Lucas was smiling again.

The photographer got off more shots before they drove away, but neither of them paid him any attention. As they turned the corner, Sophie looked over her shoulder and saw the paparazzo scrambling to get into his car.

"I think he's going to try to follow us," she said.

"*Try* being the operative word," Lucas said, easing his foot down on the accelerator.

They were close to the on-ramp for the freeway, and within seconds they were racing away at high speed, the wind whipping through their hair.

"What a dick," Sophie said after it became clear that the photographer had a snowball's chance in hell of catching them.

"No. Dicks are useful. He's a shit," Lucas said.

She shot him an amused look. "Thanks for defending my honor back there."

He shrugged. Settling down into her seat, she reached across and rested her hand on his thigh. After a few seconds, his hand pressed down over hers.

She was asleep, her head resting on his shoulder, by the time he drove up the darkened driveway of the Jenkinses' estate.

Sophie stirred and stretched as he pulled into the garage.

"That didn't take long." She yawned, pleased to be back.

"That's because you snored most of the way."

"I do not snore," she said, then she let out a yelp of surprise when he scooped her up into his arms and strode toward the house.

"Wow. I feel like there should be some stirring music playing to complete this moment," she said. "Or you should at least be wearing some kind of uniform."

Playing along, Lucas began humming the theme song to *An Officer and a Gentleman,* and Sophie was reduced to tears of laughter by the time he deposited her on the edge of the giant bath in his en suite.

Wiping the tears from her eyes, she quirked an eyebrow, silently asking why they were in the bathroom.

"It seems only fair, since I picked the shoes…" he said, and she bit her lip as he reached for a washcloth and she realized what he intended.

"You don't have to," she said.

"I want to."

Running the washcloth under a hot tap and lathering it up with soap, he knelt at her feet and placed a folded towel across his knees. Then he reached for her left foot and laid it in his lap. Sophie sighed with pure pleasure as the hot washcloth was wrapped around her aching foot.

"Ohhh, that's *so* good," she said.

Gently he soothed her whole foot, rubbing the arch firmly and massaging the ball with strong fingers. Her eyes were practically rolling back into her head with pleasure by the time he lifted her right foot and started all over again.

Watching him through half-closed eyes, she marveled that a man who had been fawned over by half of Sydney's glitterati was kneeling at her feet, treating her with such tender reverence. Tears pricked at the backs of her eyes again, and again she blinked them away.

What the hell was wrong with her tonight?

But she knew—she just didn't want to face her own feelings yet.

With her feet well and truly soothed, Lucas's hands slid up onto her calves. She closed her eyes and slumped bonelessly as he kneaded muscles unused to being flexed tight for hours on end in high heels.

"You're a god," she groaned as he found a particularly sore spot.

His touch was so persuasive, so hypnotic, that when his hands slid up onto her thighs, she let them fall wide instinctively, welcoming his touch. And when he slid her thong down her thighs and began to caress the delicate folds between her legs with first his fingers and then his mouth, she gave herself over utterly to the experience.

The feel of his mouth on her was exquisite—firm and wet and searching. Gripping the lip of the bath, she rode the waves of desire building inside her.

Just when she thought she couldn't stand another second, he stopped and carried her into the bedroom. Stripping her and himself, he kissed her long and deep as his body fitted into the welcoming cradle of her thighs and he slid slowly into her. Wrapping her legs around his waist, she pressed kisses to his lips, his neck, his chest as they rode together. And when she came, he shuddered out his climax, too. For a precious handful of seconds she felt as though their bodies really had become one.

With his weight pressing her into the bed and his heartbeat pounding in time with her own, Sophie at last had the courage to acknowledge the feelings that had been growing inside her for the past weeks. She loved

Lucas. Somehow, by slow increments, her feelings had crept around the guard she'd placed over her heart and she'd allowed herself to care for him.

It wasn't because he was a famous movie star. If anything, it was despite that. She loved the gentleness in him, the generosity, the thoughtfulness. She loved the way he laughed, the way he played so freely, the way he made her feel. She loved his talent, and his honesty, and his vulnerability—because even if Lucas would never, ever admit it, even to himself, he was terribly, achingly vulnerable. She wanted to help him face whatever ghosts were haunting him from his past, and she wanted to make it up to him for whatever loss or hurt he had suffered. She wanted to love him, wholeheart-edly, unreservedly.

And because she felt so much, because it was so un-deniable, she wanted to say it out loud, to let him know he was loved, cherished, adored. Pressing a kiss into his neck, then another onto the corner of his mouth, and yet another on the angle of his cheekbone, she made her declaration.

"I love you, Lucas," she said.

15

I LOVE YOU, Lucas.

Sophie's words seemed to hang in the air for an aeon.
Aware that his body had tensed in reaction, Lucas forced
himself to relax again and to press a kiss onto her temple
when what he really wanted to do was withdraw from
her and roll out of bed and get the hell out of here.

She loved him.

Shit.

This was the last thing that he'd wanted to happen.
He didn't want to hurt her—but he was going to, as inevitably as night followed day.

The silence between them stretched and stretched,
and Lucas closed his eyes, filled with regret. Sophie was
so warm and generous, so earthy and sensual. If ever he
was going to let himself love someone, it would be her.
But he wasn't. Or he couldn't—same thing at the end
of the day, because both roads led to heartache and disappointment for Sophie.

Because he didn't know how to respond verbally to
her brave offering, he instinctively began to caress her
again, stroking her, teasing her, building her desire. *I
didn't set out to hurt you,* he told her silently as he

smoothed a hand across her belly. *I think you're won-derful,* he told her with his hands as he cupped her breasts. *If I believed in love, if I trusted it, I would love you,* he told her as his body grew hard for her again. Then he was inside her, every stroke an unspoken homage to how beautiful she was, how funny and sweet and kind and sexy.

I'm sorry, Sophie, he told her as desire swept them away again. *I'm so, so sorry that I can't love you back.*

Afterward, she dozed in his arms, and he eased himself free of her and left her alone in his bed. Feeling like a rat, he grabbed his cell phone and walked naked into the bathroom and shut the door. Sitting hunched on the cold tile of the bath surround, he dialed Derek's message service.

"Derek, it's me. I need you to do something for me…"

SOPHIE WOKE LATE the next morning, and it took a few seconds for memory to return.

She'd told Lucas she loved him last night. She closed her eyes and winced as she recalled the way his body had tensed and the taut silence that had hung between them for too, too long after her declaration.

She'd been on the verge of making an attempt to retract or qualify her words when he'd started kissing her and touching her and she'd felt the fierce intensity in his caresses. He hadn't said he loved her, but she knew he felt something. He cared for her. The sense of connection she felt was not one-sided—and for now, perhaps that was enough. And it wasn't as though she could stop herself from loving him, anyway. If that boat was ever going to float, she wouldn't be in this situation in the first place.

She loved him. With all her heart and soul. It was a gift, and she'd bestowed it on him, foolish or not. And as embarrassing as last night's nonreturned avowal was, she was glad she'd made it. Despite all his fame and money, she suspected that Lucas Grant had had precious little real love in his life. So, now he had hers.

She wasn't really sure where that left her, of course. Falling in love with one of the world's most notorious womanizing hell-raisers wasn't exactly a guarantee of future happiness. Maybe it even made her as stupid as those other women, the ones she'd been so contemptuous of when Lucas had delivered his little postcoital coda to her after that first night.

But there was still hope in her heart as she rolled out of bed and went in search of Lucas. Grabbing a T-shirt he'd left abandoned at the foot of the bed, she tugged it over her head as she headed for the door. The clock on the bedside table told her it was past eleven—she couldn't remember the last time she'd slept in so late. As she descended the stairs, she caught the distinct scent of wood smoke in the air. Having grown up in a country town, she had a fair idea what that meant—bushfires. Not necessarily nearby, depending on the wind conditions, but she would check the national radio service nonetheless to find out what was going on.

If she hadn't been so preoccupied with wondering about the bushfires, she probably wouldn't have been quite so surprised when she entered the living room and found herself facing a room full of people. Better yet, a room full of people who were all staring at her. Her hands instinctively reached for the hem of Lucas's T-shirt and tugged it down as she recognized Derek and Adele. There was also a short, chubby man with thick, black-rimmed glasses, a stick-insect-thin brunette woman and a stunning blond-haired beauty wearing the tiniest bikinis Sophie had ever seen.

"Sophie," Derek said neutrally. "Let me introduce you. You know Adele, of course. Richard here is her husband. And this is Keira, and that's Camilla."

Keira, the hungry-looking brunette, smirked. "Hi, Sophie," she said, clearly amused by Sophie's discomfort. "I didn't recognize you from the front."

Sophie frowned. "Excuse me?"

"That's right. You probably haven't seen it yet," Derek said.

There was cold calculation in his eyes as he passed over the newspaper that was lying on the dining room table. The photo of her on Lucas's back was spread right across the front page in full color. The fact that she was wearing a thong was more than evident, as was the fact that she and Lucas were laughing, apparently devil-may-care about the whole situation. The only saving grace was that she had a tan, and that her face was only partly visible.

Grant's New Ride, the headline said.

Sophie was speechless, and horribly aware that everyone was studying her, assessing her.

"You're up," a familiar voice said.

Sophie swung around as Lucas entered from the terrace, dressed in nothing but a pair of low-riding board shorts. Stupidly, she'd forgotten that he no longer needed his crutches. Somehow, he didn't look like her Lucas without them and his bulky leg braces. Instead he looked every inch the handsome, powerful movie star he was. She almost took a step backward, she was so intimidated for a split second.

As embarrassing moments went, she figured this was way up there. For starters, she wasn't wearing a stitch under the T-shirt, and she had a feeling everyone knew it. Then there was the fact that she probably had a serious case of bed-head and pillow-face—and Keira and Camilla were the kind of stunning beauties that teenage boys risked blindness and hairy palms for. And lastly, of course, there was the fact that her ass was spread over the front page of the morning newspaper.

"These guys are going to stay for a few days, maybe the rest of the week. We've got enough supplies to feed them, yeah?" Lucas asked casually.

Sophie's belly tightened. That quickly, the rest of her alone time with Lucas evaporated. She'd been looking forward to their last few days together— even more so now that she'd acknowledged her own feelings. She knew that she'd taken him by surprise last night with her declaration. She'd wanted to talk with him, explain her feelings. Make sure that he knew he was under no obligation to her, that her love came with no strings or expectations, only hope.

Realizing that everyone was waiting for her to answer, she pulled her scattered thoughts together.

"There's plenty there. Unless anyone has special dietary requirements…?"

All she got was blank looks, so she decided to take that as a no.

"Great. Shall we say lunch at one, then?" Lucas asked.

There was something about his tone…. Sophie shot him a questioning look but his expression was blandly neutral. Maybe he was pissed about their surprise arrivals and the horrible headline. She was; it made sense that he would be.

"Sure. One o'clock is good," she said. She hesitated, wanting to bring up the newspaper, but not sure what she wanted to say. Then the need to not be standing nearly naked in a roomful of strangers took over. "I'll just go get dressed."

As she made her way up the stairs, she tried to work out what it was about Lucas's behavior that was bugging her—apart from the fact that he hadn't woken her and warned her that they had unexpected guests.

He'd seemed…distant. That was what it was. And not once had he said or done anything to indicate to his friends that he and Sophie were more than employer and employee. Although perhaps the front page of the newspaper made that kind of redundant.

She shook her doubts off. She was simply overly sensitive because of what had happened last night.

And now she would be sharing Lucas with his friends for the rest of their time together. She felt ridiculously cheated. Just when she'd worked out her own feelings and laid them on the table, they'd run out of time.

But it soon became painfully clear that she wasn't being overly sensitive at all. Expanding her planned menu for Lucas's lunch, she added some salads and side dishes, baked some fresh rolls and mixed up a jug of iced tea. All the while she cooked, she could hear laughter and music filtering from the terrace. It had been a while since she'd been in the kitchen on her own—Lucas had usually kept her company over the past few weeks, sneaking tidbits when he thought she wasn't looking— and she was surprised at how isolated she felt.

Loading up a tray with cutlery and crockery, she made her way out onto the terrace, assuming that Lucas's guests would probably want to eat alfresco since they were already by the pool. The smell of wood smoke was more intense out of doors, and she reminded herself that she still hadn't checked the radio service.

Her friendly heads-up died in her throat when she arrived at poolside and saw Lucas. Or, more accurately, Lucas and Camilla. He was sitting on one of the loungers, his thighs spread wide, Camilla, in her tiny bikini, nestling between them while he gave her a shoulder massage. The girl's dead-straight blond hair hung over her down-turned face as she gave encouraging moans. Lucas's expression was unreadable behind his dark sunglasses as he worked on her.

"Lucas, you have magic hands," Camilla groaned, rolling her shoulders encouragingly.

Sophie almost turned around. Only pride made her stick it. Crossing to the nearby table, she transferred the stack of plates and cutlery.

"Lunch won't be a moment," she said, turning back toward the house before anyone could see the pain and hurt in her face.

Derek said something she couldn't quite hear as she walked away, and Camilla laughed loudly and said something in reply.

"Oh, that's a great idea, Cam," she heard Keira say, and even though she knew it was pure self-torture, Sophie found herself looking over her shoulder just in time to see Camilla throwing her tiny bikini top to one side, baring her full, pouty breasts to the world.

"We're all friends, after all," Camilla said as Keira followed suit.

Sophie's gaze shifted toward Lucas's face, but he remained impassive behind his sunglasses.

It didn't matter. She didn't need to see his eyes to understand that he was doing this on purpose. She knew it, absolutely. She'd crossed the line last night—and Lucas was pushing her firmly back over it.

The friends arriving unexpectedly—she'd bet her life savings he'd asked them to come. As for what he was doing with Camilla... She wondered how far his fear would drive him. Would he actually sleep with the other woman to prove to Sophie that what he had with her meant nothing?

Standing alone in the kitchen, Sophie braced her hands against the counter and bowed her head for a minute.

How could something so new and fresh hurt this much?

It was crazy, but having Brandon call it quits hadn't even come close to being this painful, and she'd spent fourteen years by his side.

She didn't understand. But what she did get, loud and clear, was that Lucas didn't want her love. And Camilla and Derek and the rest of them were his way of reminding her what his relationship with her had been all about. Four weeks. Fun. No strings.

She'd gotten the message. And it broke her heart and made her angry in equal measures.

LUCAS FELT LOWER than a snake's belly. The look on Sophie's face when she'd seen him with Camilla—funny how he could remember her name now—would live with him for a long time. But he'd still done the right thing.

She'd hate him for it, of course. The sooner she fell out of love with him the better.

"Lucas, come swim. It's perfect," Camilla called, bobbing up and down in the water so that her breasts jiggled invitingly.

He couldn't be less interested. She was a beautiful woman—but she wasn't Sophie. And while Sophie might not have legs till Tuesday and cheekbones to die for, she had fifty million times more appeal. Thinking of her big cinnamon eyes, her full lips, the sound of her laughter made him feel like a rat all over again. He'd hurt her today, deliberately. She'd never been anything but open and honest with him—and he'd repaid her with deceit and disrespect. What kind of a heel did that make him? Even if he was doing it for her own good?

"I've got some stuff to take care of," he said. He couldn't hang out here by the pool, pretending to have a good time when Sophie had just been kicked in the teeth. Especially when he'd been the one to do the kicking.

Levering himself to his feet, he made his way inside. Predictably, he found Sophie in the kitchen, the radio on beside her as she cut up greens for a salad. She didn't look up straight away, even though she couldn't fail to be aware of his presence, and the radio announcer's smooth tones filled the silence between them.

"…fire authorities are working around the clock to clear fire breaks. With a prevailing northerly wind predicted, police have started doing the rounds in the Blue Mountain townships of Bullaburra, Lawson and Hazelbrook to start evacuation plans…"

When the announcer moved on to other news, Sophie reached across to switch the radio off. Only then did she make eye contact with him. He almost flinched from the raw hurt he saw in her gaze.

"You could have just said thanks, but no thanks, Sophie. You didn't need to bring all these people up here," she said. "You definitely didn't have to put on a show with some bikini babe."

There was something about having his actions laid bare on the table that made Lucas feel distinctly small.

"We both knew what this was," he said. "I warned you I wasn't a one-woman guy. I made it very clear that I don't do commitment." He sounded defensive—probably because that was how he felt.

"I get that. But the least you owed me was a conversation. A little bit of consideration. Is that too much to ask?"

It wasn't, but it was. He stared at her, wanting to comfort her, to apologize, but knowing that he had nothing to offer and that her anger was going to be the best cure for her feelings for him.

"It scares you, doesn't it? Me loving you?" she asked quietly. "The fact that I can be honest and up-front about it. I bet if I took your pulse right now it would be through the roof."

Ignoring the fact that she was right and his heart was pounding against his rib cage and his palms were sweaty, Lucas bristled.

"Listen, I'm sorry things haven't worked out the way you wanted. I like you, Sophie. I think you're great. But that's all," he said.

"And what about your nightmares? They don't mean anything, as well, I take it?"

Jesus, they were back to this again.

"Spare me the psychobabble," he said. "This is not about me."

"Isn't it? Let me tell you just how much this is about you, Lucas. You're a grown man who experiences the same nightmare from his childhood over and over yet refuses to deal with it. You're a man who has deliberately avoided making a home for himself anywhere in the world or forming meaningful connections with people—you even hate your own manager, for Pete's sake. You make a living by pretending to be other people. And when I have the temerity, the gall, to tell you that I love you, your first response is to create a situation where I will be so repulsed, so hurt that I will retract my offering and retreat. This is so much about you it's not funny."

Perhaps it was the mention of his nightmares, or maybe it was the crack about him being afraid of intimacy. Whatever—he saw red.

"I'm sorry, Sophie, but it's not my fault that you wasted the last fourteen years of your life with Mr.

Bland because you were freaking out over your sister," he said. "Don't try to pin any of this on me. I didn't ask for you to fall in love me."

She stared at him. "Why are you being so cruel?"

He couldn't hold her eye.

"You're the one who made this messy, Sophie."

"Because I fell in love with you? What a crime," she said, then she turned on her heel.

"You can cook your own lunch," she said over her shoulder as she exited.

Lucas stood alone in the kitchen, staring at the blank wall for a long time.

It was done. Time to move on.

16

SOPHIE COULDN'T BELIEVE that the same man who had tenderly washed her feet last night had just flirted with some topless bimbo right in front of her. And she couldn't believe that he'd made that crack about her and Brandon. Alone in the caretaker's lodge, Sophie paced, needing to find an outlet for all the anger bubbling up inside her.

He was so closed off, so self-protective. While she understood why a kid growing up the way he did might find it necessary to guard himself like that, it made her so mad when she thought about what he was turning his back on.

And she wasn't only thinking of her own love for him. She was thinking about all the other ordinary connections with human beings that he denied himself all the time, using his playboy persona to keep the world at a distance. Over the past few weeks he'd let his guard down and allowed her to see the real Lucas. It was why she'd fallen deeply, profoundly in love with him. But he hated being that vulnerable. And he refused to let love into his life.

And the best, the most stellar thing about all of it was

that he was so famous that even if she never saw him again in the flesh, she'd be confronted by his image on billboards, in magazines and on cinema screens for the rest of her life.

Sophie slumped onto the couch and put her head in her hands.

What made her saddest of all was the fact that she would never get the chance to chase the shadows out from behind his eyes. She wanted to care for him, help him heal, love him. She wanted to wake up with his body curled around hers, his breath on the back of her neck. She wanted to hear him laugh every day, and beat him at Scrabble and do a hundred thousand more crosswords with him.

Four weeks was not enough. It was never going to be enough—something she'd known instinctively right from the start. Something she now had a lifetime to regret.

The tears came then. Body-racking sobs that made her stomach and chest hurt. She wound up on the bed, curled into her knees, howling like a bereft child. It was such a loss—to have found the special man beneath all that surface charm, only to lose him just as she was beginning to finally understand him. It seemed profoundly unfair. And it hurt—it hurt with a physical ache in her heart.

She loved Lucas Grant, and he did not or could not love her in return.

Dinnertime came and went. She figured they could order in food if they wanted to eat. Eventually she fell asleep, and the face that greeted her the next morning was pale and puffy-eyed.

Great. Now she had to make breakfast for the beautiful people looking like a slit-eyed goblin. Joy to the world.

She was surprised to find a thick pall of smoke hanging over the estate when she exited the lodge. The bushfires had obviously grown worse in the night. Her step brisk, she headed for the radio in the kitchen.

She stopped in her tracks when she saw the stack of luggage just inside the door from the terrace. Since it was large and expensive-looking, she figured it was Lucas's. Continuing through to the kitchen, she found him leaning against the counter eating a bowl of cereal.

"You're leaving."

"We all are. They're issuing warnings for this area now. The wind changed overnight and the fire is into the state forest."

Sophie nodded. "I see. Well, that makes it easy then, doesn't it?"

She could feel his gaze on her, and she wished for her pride's sake that she didn't look as though she'd been crying her heart out half the night.

"Are you all right?" he asked. She could hear the reluctance in his tone, and it made her toes curl. The last thing she wanted was his pity.

"I'm fine," she said, busying herself at the fridge. If they were evacuating, she needed to dispose of any perishables.

"You don't look fine," he said.

"Thank you. I'm aware of that."

He hovered for a few more minutes, but she ignored him. Only when he turned his back did she look at him, her eyes mapping the width of his shoulders, the length of his legs as he exited the kitchen.

He was so handsome, so appealing. And she was such a fool for falling for him.

By the time she'd filled two cartons with fresh produce and given the kitchen a quick clean, Derek, Adele and friends had gone and only Lucas was left. He caught up to her as she lugged the first of the produce boxes to her car. His Porsche was sitting in the driveway, the roof up in deference to the smoke haze.

"Let me take that," he said, reaching for the box.

She twisted her hips, jerking the box from his grasp. "I can handle it."

Spine straight, she marched around the back of the garage to where she'd parked her faded green Volkswagen.

"How much longer are you going to be?" Lucas asked from behind her, and Sophie dropped the carton into the trunk of her car with a thump.

"You know, you should just go," she suggested. "I need to pack up my stuff and make sure I didn't leave anything up in your room."

"I'm asking because I think the smoke is getting thicker, not because I'm hassling you," he said.

"If things were that dicey, the police would have come knocking to clear us out. I grew up in the country," she said. "I know the drill."

He eyed her uncertainly, his gaze shifting over her shoulder to consider the smoke haze. Staring up at his strong, handsome face, she was overwhelmed by a pathetic, weak urge to throw herself at his feet and beg him to at least give them a chance.

"Be careful, Lucas. Any more of this and I might get the idea that you care or something," she said, mostly because she wanted him to go before she did or said something irredeemably feeble. "I can look after myself, you know."

"Fine. If that's what you want," he said. He slid his sunglasses on, and she found herself staring at a warped, double reflection of her own face in his lenses and had to look away from the pain she saw there.

"I had a good time, Sophie," he said quietly.

"Sure." The single word was all she could manage. She was too busy swallowing stupid tears to muster anything else.

He hesitated a moment, then walked away.

She waited until she heard the sound of his car engine firing before she headed toward the house.

Goodbye, Lucas. It was nice loving you.

LUCAS PUT HIS FOOT to the floor and took the turns in the mountain road way too quickly.

He felt like shit. He'd hurt Sophie. He'd left her alone to close up the house. He hadn't had the courage to say any of the things that he wanted to say to her. Such as, if ever he was going to take the risk of loving someone, it would be her. And he missed her laughter. And he would never forget her or the time they'd spent together.

"Damn it," he swore, thumping the steering wheel with a closed fist.

He slowed, tempted to pull onto the verge and execute a U-turn. It felt wrong to be driving away from her like this.

But if he went back, what was he going to say to her? What did he have to offer?

He couldn't ask her to continue their relationship on a casual basis, no matter how much he was going to miss her, no matter how much he wanted to be near her. She loved him, which meant she was out of bounds. He would only hurt her further if he selfishly pursued his own desires.

He thumped the steering wheel again as he thought about the things she'd said to him last night about his nightmares and his career choice and his lifestyle. He was a successful guy. He had money, fame, power. Yet she'd made him sound so small and hollow.

Which just went to show how little she knew about him, and how dangerous a little psychological double-speak could be in the wrong hands.

One thing she'd said kept niggling at him, however: that he was afraid of intimacy. Her implication that he surrounded himself with people he didn't really like or trust had gnawed at him all night. Especially because she'd cited Derek as an example.

Because it was true. Lucas didn't like his manager. He and Derek didn't share the same values, or the same sense of who Lucas was as an actor. They didn't even have the same vision for his career. He'd told himself over and over that he tolerated Derek's greed, insensitivity and slick insincerity because having a manager in Hollywood was a necessary evil, and Derek was no more or less sleazy than the next guy or gal.

But it wasn't true, and he knew it. So why did he tolerate the relationship?

And why had he not missed a single one of his "friends" while he'd been sequestered in the mountains with Sophie for almost a month? When he was in Sydney or L.A. or New York, he could be busy every night of the week if he so chose. So why hadn't he felt the itch to make contact with any of his usual social circle?

And perhaps most tellingly, why did a beautiful girl like Camilla—a woman he'd been hot for less than a month ago—leave him cold now that he'd experienced the warmth of having Sophie in his world?

His foot pressed harder on the accelerator as he tried to outrun his thoughts. He'd get over her. It had just been four weeks of fun, after all.

The words rang hollow, even to him, but the sound of sirens distracted him. He edged the Porsche closer to the side of the road as three huge fire trucks raced past, heading up the mountain. Slowing even more, Lucas watched them disappear into the smoke haze in the rearview mirror. Flicking on the car radio, he roamed around until he found Radio National. He was drumming his fingers impatiently on the steering wheel, waiting for a bushfire update, when he rounded a hairpin turn and found himself driving toward a roadblock.

The two police officers staffing it waved him through, but Lucas braked to a halt and let his window down.

"Hey. What's going on back up the mountain?" he asked.

The cop's eyes widened as he recognized him.

"Wow. Hi," he said, his mouth twisting into a goofy smile.

Lucas sighed. "Up the mountain?" he prompted again, jerking his thumb over his shoulder.

"Yeah. Right. The fire's jumped the breaks again. We're evacuating everything west of here."

"Where's the fire front?" Lucas asked, his gut tightening.

Sophie was still back up there somewhere.

"Coming through Faulconbridge and Linden, last we heard."

Both only twenty minutes by car from the Jenkinses' estate. Bushfires could travel quickly, he knew from watching decades of news reports. Which meant Sophie could be trapped back there, either at the house or on the road.

He didn't stop to think, he just acted. Slamming the car into reverse, he executed a swerving three-point turn. The cop raced forward, a frown on his previously starstruck face.

"Lucas, mate, what are you doing?" he asked, grabbing the car door as though he could physically prevent Lucas from leaving.

"I've got a friend back up there," Lucas said.

"You can't go back. The fire crews are up there. We'll radio them and tell them to be on the alert," the cop offered.

"Not good enough," Lucas said.

And it wasn't. Not when Sophie was in danger. He wasn't leaving her up there to face a raging bushfire on her own. Ignoring the cop's shout of protest, he gunned the motor and the car sprang forward. Within seconds the roadblock behind him had been swallowed by the smoke haze.

Flicking his high beams on, Lucas took the first

corner at speed. Reaching for his cell, he found Julie Jenkins's number. She answered on the first ring.

"Julie, it's Lucas Grant. I need Sophie Gallagher's cell number. Do you have it?" he asked, not bothering with social niceties.

"Lucas—I was just about to call you. Please tell me you and Sophie have evacuated the house," she asked.

"I'm on my way back there right now, but I don't know if Sophie's left," he explained.

Julie was a smart woman, and she didn't waste another second of his time as she reeled off Sophie's number. He ended the call with a brisk thanks and punched in Sophie's number. When it went straight through to voice mail, he swore.

"Sophie, if you're still at the house, stay there. The front is coming through. Stay indoors, and find a room where you can protect yourself from smoke," he instructed.

Throwing his phone onto the passenger seat, he concentrated on the road. The smoke was getting thicker and thicker, and twice he passed cars speeding in the opposite direction. Neither of them was Sophie's green Beetle, and he gripped the wheel harder as he tried not to think about why she would have been so delayed in following him off the mountain.

His answer came soon enough. Cresting a rise, his headlights picked out a dark shape in the eddying smoke up ahead. He eased back on the gas as he made out the distinctive curved shape of her car. A small figure was hunkered down beside it, working furiously to change a flat tire.

"Jesus," he swore under his breath. Thank God he'd come back.

Swerving his car onto the verge, he pulled the car into a sharp U-turn and parked it, pointing down the mountain, ready for a fast exit. Leaving the engine running, he shoved open the car door and ran across to where Sophie was standing, squinting at him through the smoke.

"Get in the car," he said. "The fire's coming through."

"I know. I saw the trucks."

He grabbed her arm, urging her toward the Porsche.

"I can't. My car…" she said, digging her heels in.

"I'll buy you a new one," he said, his only thought to get her to safety.

"No, wait!" she said, tugging her arm free from his grasp and spinning back toward the Beetle.

He leaped after her, but she already had the car door open, and he saw she was collecting a carton from the passenger seat. Lord help him, but if she was trying to save the groceries, he was going to shake her till her teeth rattled!

Then she straightened and he saw the curled form of a baby wombat nestling in among Sophie's chef's clothes and recipe folder.

"I found him wandering on the road," Sophie said, her big eyes anxious. "I couldn't leave him up there. If the fire didn't get him, he'd probably get squished by a truck."

Only Sophie could risk life and limb for a ball of fur with an oversize nose.

"You are unbelievable," he said. "Come on."

They'd barely taken a step toward his waiting car when they heard it—an intense roaring like a jet airplane about to take off. A surge of intense heat hit them, and they both began to cough as the smoke around them became thick and dark.

The fire front was on them. Sophie gave a start of fright as a big red kangaroo burst from the bush nearby, racing for its life as the fire chased it.

"Down!" Lucas yelled over the roar, shoving Sophie back toward her car. The Porsche was only meters away, but even that was too far under the circumstances. There wasn't even time to get inside her car and roll up the windows. Instead, he thrust Sophie to the ground in the lee of her car, snatching her chef's coat from the wombat's box and covering her head and face with it. She slid the box as close to the car as possible, curling her body around it, and he lay over top of her, covering as much of her as he could.

Then it hit them. A roaring, crackling, searing monster that leaped the narrow roadway with voracious hunger. He didn't dare lift his head. All he could do was hope that the car afforded them enough shelter to outlast the intense heat of the front as it passed. In theory, with a canopy fire like this one, that should only take a matter of seconds, maybe minutes.

He could feel Sophie's body trembling with fear beneath his, and he gripped her tight, trying to reassure her wordlessly. If anything were to happen to her... He didn't want to think about a world without Sophie in it.

Somehow her hand found his, and they gripped each other in terror as the fire roared around them. His back stung from the heat, and he pressed his face closer to

Sophie's nape, concentrating on her smell, on the feel of her beneath him, on how precious and generous and funny she was.

That was when it hit him, with more force than a thousand bushfires. He loved her. Despite all attempts to keep her at arm's length, despite his lifelong mistrust of love and all it entailed, he'd fallen in love with Sophie Gallagher.

He was still reeling from the realization when the heat eased and the roar of the fire died. All in all, the front had taken less than a minute to pass, but they had been the most profound sixty seconds of Lucas's life.

He clenched his fingers into the fabric of Sophie's jeans as he thought about how close he'd come to losing her. If she'd been caught out alone, changing her tire… If he'd kept driving and not turned around…

He wanted to protect her with every fiber of his being. He wanted to wrap her tight and never let her go again. He loved her. Against every self-protective instinct he had, he loved her.

"I think it's passed," she said, her voice muffled.

She wriggled, indicating she wanted him to let her go, and Lucas forced himself to unclench his fingers and roll away from her. The tarmac was hot from the fire and he winced and quickly sat upright, coughing in the still-thick smoke.

"We should go, in case the wind changes again," Sophie said.

She kept her face down, and he used a finger to tip her chin up so he could see her expression.

"Are you okay?" he asked.

She grimaced and held out a hand to show him it was trembling.

"Apart from seeing my life flash before my eyes, sure."

"Come on."

He grabbed the wombat box and they crossed to the Porsche. It had survived the fire intact, give or take a little blistered paint. Sophie slid into the passenger seat and he passed her the box before getting behind the wheel.

He drove more cautiously, remembering the kangaroo's headlong rush from the bush. The last thing they needed was a close encounter with a hundred-and-fifty-pound 'roo. All the while, his thoughts churned over and over, circling around the profound revelation the fire had brought him.

Unfamiliar words choked his throat, but he held on to them until they'd cleared the police block and made it to the lowlands, well beyond the reach of the fires.

His gut tight with apprehension, Lucas pulled over onto the side of the road at the first rest stop he found. Cutting the engine, he turned to face Sophie.

She stared at him, eyebrows raised, one hand resting protectively on the wombat's furry body.

"Is something wrong?" she asked.

He swallowed and said the words he'd always promised himself he never would.

"Sophie, I love you."

_17_

LUCAS'S WORDS SEEMED to echo around the interior of the car. Sophie stared at him, noting the way he gripped the steering wheel as though his life depended on it, and the frantic, giveaway pulse beating at the base of his neck.

He's terrified, she realized. Absolutely terrified.

"You love me," she repeated slowly, not quite ready to let herself believe it yet. It was what she wanted to hear, more than anything. But he looked as though he was about to face a firing squad.

"When I thought you were trapped back there… When the fire front came through… All I could think of was protecting you. And how much you mean to me," he said.

His grip on the steering wheel was white-knuckled now. Sophie frowned, keeping a tight rein on the hope blooming in her heart. This wasn't exactly the declaration of an open and loving man. But she already knew that about Lucas, didn't she? That intimacy and love were difficult things for him.

"You know how I feel about you," she said quietly.

He nodded. "Yes. Which kind of leaves us in an interesting position."

"Does it?" she asked carefully. "How so?"

All she wanted him to do was kiss her. Kiss her and hold her and look into her eyes and tell her he loved her as though it was something to celebrate.

"We need to work out what happens next. How this might pan out," he said.

She frowned, not understanding. "We spend time with each other. We enjoy each other. We build on the love we both feel," she said.

"Sure. Okay. I guess what I'm thinking is that I move around a lot. It's going to be hard to make this work."

"We're resourceful. We can find a way," she said.

Why wasn't he just kissing her, for Pete's sake? Why were they even having this conversation?

"I guess you could travel with me, but I don't want to drag you away from your life. It'll make it harder afterward."

Sophie narrowed her eyes. "After what?"

He shrugged, avoiding her gaze.

Suddenly she got it.

"You mean after it's over, don't you? After we break up?" she asked.

"Yeah. I guess."

The hope in her heart shriveled before it had a chance to fully flower. She'd thought that hearing Lucas say the words would be enough, knowing that he was willing to risk loving her and all that that entailed. But how could they have a relationship when he was already looking toward an end date? What kind of a foundation was that for them to build on?

She stared at him, her gaze traveling over his beautiful features. Did he really think he was that unlovable? Had his childhood damaged him so deeply, so irreparably that he could never truly trust another person with his vulnerability?

She wanted to reach out and hold him and reassure him with everything in her that she loved him and she wasn't going anywhere. She wanted to move heaven and earth to convey the depth of her feeling for him. But she knew in her heart of hearts that it would never be enough—not if Lucas couldn't come to terms with his past.

"No," she said, shaking her head.

"No, what?" he asked.

"No, we're not doing this. We're not going into some kind of half-assed, grudging, reluctant relationship based on fear and the anticipation of failure," she said firmly.

He stared at her. "That's not what I was suggesting," he said stiffly.

"Yeah, it was. You think we're going to fail before we've even started. You don't even want to love me, do you? You love me despite yourself. Admit it to yourself, even if you won't admit it to me," she said.

She felt very calm, very sure all of a sudden. She'd wasted years of her life with Brandon for the wrong reasons. She could try to make things work with Lucas, try to outlast his uncertainty and caution. But she deserved better. And, at the end of the day, so did Lucas.

If they were ever going to have a future, he needed to understand his past. She turned to face him fully, twisting awkwardly with the wombat box in her lap. Capturing both his hands, she held them in her own.

"If we're going to do this, Lucas, you need to deal

with your childhood," she said bluntly. "I don't know what form that might take—talking to someone, talking to me, whatever. But you can't keep squashing it into a corner and pretending it's not there anymore."

His expression darkened and he shook his head automatically.

"Will you let all that stuff go, Sophie? It was shitty, but it's over. I've moved on. I want to move on with you," he said, his voice growing in confidence as he talked himself into it.

Sophie took a deep breath and took the gamble of her life.

"I can't be with you if you won't deal with this, Lucas. It's no way to start a life together."

He flinched, his frown deepening. "Is that— Is that an ultimatum?" he asked her incredulously.

She stared at him, then slowly nodded. "Yeah, I guess it is."

They stared at each other in silence. She could see the anger in him, the frustration he felt at having risked enough to declare himself to her, only to have her set the bar even higher. Almost, she relented—but she knew that his past would haunt them forever unless he dealt with it.

Without saying a word, he started the car again and pulled back out into traffic. Sophie's stomach danced with nerves as she waited for him to say something, say anything. Surely she hadn't misjudged him? He'd been willing to acknowledge his love, surely he would be prepared to acknowledge his past if she was standing by his side, helping him every step of the way?

He waited a full ten minutes, and when he spoke it was calm and measured.

"I love you. I want to be with you. Why isn't that enough?" he said.

If he'd said the exact same thing to her last night, she would have thrown herself into his arms. But she knew what she was up against now. She'd seen the depths of his fear when he'd used Derek and Camilla to push her away.

"If it's not a problem, talking about it shouldn't be a big deal," she pointed out quietly.

"It's not up for grabs," he said, his tone clipped, no-nonsense.

She stared at his profile. She felt sick about what she was about to say, but she had to stick to her guns. She knew she would be letting him down if she didn't.

"Then you know my answer."

His jaw tensed, and the car picked up speed. For the remaining half hour of the drive to her apartment, neither of them said a word. A dozen times Sophie opened her mouth to retract her challenge. But each time she bit her tongue. She wanted all of him, not the small portion of himself that he was willing to risk. Maybe that made her greedy, even stupid, to risk so much, but she wanted him to love her as openly as she loved him. And if the past hour had taught her anything, it was that he was nowhere near ready to do that. But she hadn't given up hope yet.

Parking out in front of her apartment, he carried the wombat up the stairs for her. She took it from him in the hallway and slid it inside her open door, then turned to face him.

"I love you so much, Lucas. Please try for us," she said.

His face creased with confusion, and she caught a flash of fear in his eyes. "Then why are you making this harder than it needs to be?"

"Because I want to set you free of that nightmare," she said. "Can't you understand that?"

He stared at her, his jaw clenched. She stood on tiptoes and pressed a kiss to his lips. His hands came up and cupped her face as he deepened the kiss, his tongue stroking hers, his body moving closer, seeking comfort and heat.

He nudged a knee between hers, one hand sliding onto her butt to encourage her into close contact with his thigh. The other hand slid up her ribs and found her breasts. The familiar need built inside her, but she forced herself to slide her hands between them and push him away. She knew exactly how charming he was, and how susceptible she was to that charm. She needed to stay strong.

"Think about it. Don't give me your answer now," she said, taking a step away from him.

"My answer's not going to change, Sophie," he said, and she heard the finality in his voice.

She stared at him for a long, long beat. This was her moment of choice, then—take what he was offering, or walk away. She loved him so much, it was tempting to take the crumbs from his table. But she knew she would wind up so wounded, so hurt at the end of the day. The pain she felt now would be nothing compared to how she'd feel when she was forced to walk away from him in six months, a year, two years because Lucas was too closed off to invest in their relationship.

"Then I guess this is goodbye."

He looked shocked for a second. Then a shuttered expression slid over his face and she lost all sight of his emotions.

Without saying another word, he turned on his heel and left.

She stared after him, even took a step to chase him. But she stopped before she'd really started, tears welling in her eyes as she registered that she may have just made the biggest mistake of her life.

Lucas went home to his stark, white house and went straight into the gym. Ignoring his doctor's instructions to take it easy on his newly healed knee and ankle, he pulled on a pair of workout pants and trainers and hit the treadmill.

He ran, his feet pounding the track, his body falling into a familiar rhythm despite the long break in his training.

He wasn't prepared to give up on Sophie. He hadn't waited thirty-five years to fall in love for the first time, only to walk away at the last hurdle. She had a bee in her bonnet over his nightmares, but he knew from experience that they would pass. He just had to wait them out, and they'd fade away. He was confident that if he could show her that, convince her of it, then they could take up where they'd left off.

Slowly a plan formed in his mind as his muscles warmed and his body loosened.

Sophie loved him. And he'd already charmed her into bed once. He could do it again—hell, everything was in his favor, after all. And once he had her naked, he'd make sure she never walked away again.

By the time he'd burned up an hour on the tread-mill, his churning thoughts had settled into ordered determination.

The next morning he sent her flowers and a case of French champagne. He waited till the end of the day to follow up with a phone call.

"Come to dinner with me," he said.

"What are we going to talk about?" she asked.

He frowned. "Sophie…"

"Then my answer is no." And she hung up on him.

The next day he sent chocolates and a box of organic fruit and vegetables, then turned up in person to seduce her into coming out on a date. She answered the door wearing a pair of purple flannel pyjamas with monkeys on them and a floppy sweatshirt, and he got hard on the spot.

"Come out with me," he said, leaning one hand on the doorframe and eyeing her beautiful breasts hungrily

"As soon as we talk about your parents."

He growled and straightened, throwing his hands in the air in frustration.

"I have no memory of them," he said. "I was made a ward of the state when I was four years old. They mean nothing to me."

"I wish that were true," she said, and she shut the door in his face.

He stared at the bright red wood and kicked it, hard. "Sophie!"

She didn't answer, and he was forced to walk away.

He tried silence for a few days before following up with another visit to her doorstep. When she didn't respond to his knocks, he charmed her neighbor into revealing Sophie had gone to stay with her parents.

Effectively removing herself from his sphere of influence. When he returned to his place, Derek was waiting for him, a glass of Lucas's best scotch in hand.

"I've got next week's shooting schedule for you," Derek said. "And there's a new three-picture offer on the table for you with Paramount. It's a nice price. I think you'll be happy."

"Look, can we talk about this later?" Lucas said, running a hand through his hair. Derek was the last person he wanted to see right now.

Derek tossed back some of the scotch. "They're giving you director and producer approval, although I had to fight for the last one. You can also develop your own projects, if you want."

"Derek. Not now," Lucas warned.

Derek's expression turned pissy. "If not now, when? You've been zoned out ever since you got back, and I've been holding these guys off for weeks already."

"I don't care," Lucas said.

"You *don't care.* Since when did you not care about your career?" Derek asked, incredulous.

Lucas crossed to the bar and poured himself a drink. Derek snorted as though he'd just worked something out.

"Please tell me this is not about the quirky little redhead," his manager asked. "Please tell me that's not why your head is up your ass at the moment, Lucas."

Lucas shot him a dark look and took a pull from his drink.

"You're freakin' kidding me," Derek said, shaking his head in disbelief. "You've lost it over the chef. This is priceless."

"I really don't want to get into it," Lucas warned him.

"Buddy, you'll get over her, don't worry. Let me call Keira or Camilla up. Hell, let me call them both. Once you've exorcised the ghost, so to speak, things will be back to normal."

Derek was already reaching for his mobile. Lucas studied him. He'd already acknowledged that he didn't like this man. So why on earth was he paying him large sums of money every year?

Not a single good reason leaped to mind.

"Derek?"

The other man looked up, finger poised over the call button on his phone.

"You're fired," Lucas said.

Derek's eyes bugged for a second. "What?"

"You heard me. I'll pay out your contract, or whatever we have that binds us together. You'll get your cut of any deals you've brokered. But I don't want you in my life anymore."

Derek's face flushed a dull red. "What about our relationship? All the years I've put in for you?"

"You're a rich guy. Throw a party," Lucas said, crossing to the front door.

Flinging it open, he waited for Derek to leave.

"You'll regret this," Derek said.

Lucas just eyed him silently, and Derek slid his glass onto the nearest flat surface and strode toward the door.

"Wait a minute," Lucas said as Derek was almost out of range.

Derek turned around, a look of intense satisfaction on his face. Clearly he thought Lucas had had second thoughts.

"Your house key, please," Lucas said, holding out his hand.

Derek's expression soured abruptly. Pulling a key ring from his pocket, he slid off a number of keys and threw them onto the pathway between them.

"Go screw yourself, Grant," he said.

Then he was gone.

Collecting his keys, Lucas went inside and set himself to the task of finding Sophie's parents' phone number. Eventually he tracked it down via Julie Jenkins, who'd bullied it from a reluctant Brandon.

The woman who answered his call sounded like Sophie, but subtly different. How Sophie would sound in thirty years' time, maybe.

"Mrs. Gallagher, it's Lucas Grant calling. I was wondering if I could speak with Sophie," he said.

"I'm sorry, but Sophie doesn't want to talk to you."

Lucas mouthed a swearword and tried to ignore the increasing feeling of desperation growing in his gut.

"Tell her I sacked Derek. Can you do that? I'll wait," he said.

She made a doubtful noise, then he heard her put the phone down. It seemed like a long wait before the phone was picked up again.

"I'm sorry, Mr. Grant. Sophie asked me to tell you to stop calling, please," Mrs. Gallagher said. She managed to sound both firm and regretful at once. "I think that's probably for the best, don't you agree?"

The next thing he knew, Lucas was listening to the dial tone.

Sophie was locking him out. Squeezing his eyes tightly shut, he rubbed the bridge of his nose.

His parents. His childhood. She wanted him to face it, stare it in the eye and come to terms with it.

Just the thought of it made his chest tighten with anxiety.

"Damn you, Sophie," he said under his breath.

For the first time in his adult life, he admitted to himself that he was afraid of his past. He didn't believe in love because he'd never had it, because the two people who were supposed to love him no matter what abandoned him to the state's care and never came looking for him.

Fourteen years in and out of foster care and state homes hadn't taught him any different. People were unreliable. It had been proven to him over and over, a thousand different ways: the foster family who had returned him to care because he was "too troubled"; the couple who'd wanted to make his arrangement permanent—until she'd gotten pregnant with their own child; the worker at the state home who'd helped himself to his charges' allowances and abused the younger children.

Lucas's life had taught him early on that he had to protect himself, and that the best relationships were built on mutual benefit, not love or trust. Yet Sophie was asking him to trust her wholeheartedly. To share himself with her utterly. To believe in a future.

Tears pricked the backs of his eyes as he acknowledged how much he wanted to be able to do all those things with her. When he thought of his life before he'd met her, it seemed so thin and empty. She'd brought sunshine into his days, and generosity of spirit. She'd taught him to care.

She deserved more than what he'd offered her. He winced as he remembered the way he'd confessed his love, the tight, controlled, scared offer he'd made her. She'd never held anything back from him—how could he offer her anything less than everything he had?

Reaching for the scotch bottle, he poured himself a hefty glassful. Taking the bottle with him, he went out onto his terrace and stared unseeingly at the harbor. The day waned, and so did the bottle. By eight in the evening, he was so drunk he could barely stand. Lying on a lounger, staring up at the night sky, Lucas made a decision that terrified him. But he'd never been a man to do anything by halves, not when he put his mind to it.

And Sophie deserved the best.

_18_

A MONTH LATER, Sophie gave up on pushing around the last few mouthfuls of porridge left in her bowl and stared out the window of her new apartment. In Rose Bay, it was smaller and cheaper than the apartment she'd shared with Brandon, but it was all hers and she'd grown to love it over the past few weeks. Well, as much as she could love anything while she was seeing the world through the monochrome filter of a broken heart.

Sighing deeply, she pulled her pyjama-clad knees closer to her chest and rested her chin on them as she stared at her neighbor's pool.

Four weeks since she'd seen or heard from Lucas. Four long, lonely, horrible, endless weeks.

Not a day had gone by when she didn't pick up the phone and think about calling him. She hadn't—so far. But her will was weakening. For starters, her body craved his touch to the point where she was seriously worried she'd become some kind of nymphomaniac. Every night she dreamed of sex. Amazing, fulfilling, moan-inducing sex with Lucas that left her feeling so…empty when she woke up that she was getting to the point where she dreaded going to sleep at night.

Had she done the right thing? At the time she'd been so sure that Lucas just needed a firm, loving push to get him to face his demons. Even when he walked away from her apartment door after she'd said no to his half-a-loaf offer, she'd been convinced she still stood a chance of finding happiness with him. And he'd proved her right, to a point, pursuing her all that week with offerings and phone calls and unexpected visits. Then she'd removed herself from temptation and gone to visit her parents. And after one last phone call to tell her he'd sacked Derek, she'd had nothing but silence.

He'd given up. She'd made it too hard for him. She'd gambled and lost.

Sighing again, she rubbed her cheek against the soft cotton of her pyjamas. She missed him so much. The glint he got in his eyes when he was about to do something outrageous. The tenderness of his touch. The sharpness of his mind.

He had a new movie coming out next month. And she knew from the celebrity magazines that he'd finished shooting on the film that had been delayed by his leg injury. He was probably back in L.A. by now. Or on the set of his next film. He'd probably forgotten her in the arms of another woman. Why not, after all? The whole of the Western world was his for the taking. Why would he feel her loss for longer than a week or two?

The sound of the telephone cut across her pity party, and she leaned across to pluck the portable receiver from the coffee table.

"Sophie, turn on the TV." It was Becky, her voice vibrating with excitement.

"Hi, Becks. Is this about going to the movies tonight? Because I'm not sure if I—"

"Just turn the TV on. Now," Becky ordered urgently.

"Becky—"

"Turn on the freaking TV, Sophie," Becky yelled down the phone.

"All right. Man, this had better be good," Sophie grumbled, scooping up the TV remote. "What station?"

"Nine. 'The Sheri Malcolm Hour,'" Becky said.

The screen sprang to life and Sophie found herself looking at a close-up of Lucas's face and caught the tail end of what he was saying.

"...not something I felt comfortable talking about previously," he said.

Sophie's chest tightened and she bit her bottom lip as she looked at his beautiful face.

"Becky, thanks for the heads-up, but I can't do this," she said, her thumb hovering on the off button.

Becky had been great ever since Sophie had returned from the mountains. It had only taken her a few days to break down and confess what had happened between her and Lucas. After she'd stopped rolling on the floor with jealousy, Becky had passed Sophie tissues and bought ice cream and generally been the best. As always.

"Don't you dare turn it off. Listen to what he's saying, Sophie," Becky said.

On screen, the camera pulled back to reveal Sheri Malcolm sitting opposite Lucas in a matching plush-cushioned armchair. In her mid-forties, Sheri was an attractive brunette and her morning chat show was a ratings winner. She was well known for her in-depth celebrity interviews, and right now she was eyeing Lucas as if he'd just tipped a treasure chest of gold bullion into her lap.

"You've thrown me, Lucas, I have to be honest. I mean, you're notorious for being tight-lipped about your personal life. Every time you come on here you let me know there are certain aspects of your life that aren't up for grabs," Sheri said.

"And there still are. But something happened recently that made me understand that maybe I'd been keeping quiet for the wrong reasons."

"And this realization sent you in search of your family?" Sheri asked. "Is that right?"

"Yes."

"And what did you find?" Sheri asked.

Sophie couldn't believe Lucas was doing this. It was hard for him, too—she could see it in the stiffness of his shoulders and the way his hands gripped his knees.

"I discovered that the truth was much less frightening and awful than anything I had imagined over the years." Lucas gave a self-deprecating laugh. "Kids in care imagine a lot of stuff about how they got there, why there's no one who's prepared to take them on. I always told myself I didn't care why my parents had dumped me."

"But you did," Sheri said quietly.

"Yeah. Of course I did. I was a kid. I wanted a mom and dad like everyone else. I wanted Christmas day and a dog and a bike to ride up and down the street."

"And can you tell us what happened with your parents?" Sheri asked.

Sophie pressed a hand to her mouth. Surely he wasn't going to tell the world?

"My mother died. She was English, traveling through Australia on her own, apparently. There's no record of my father. They couldn't find any relatives to take me on, so I became a ward of the state," Lucas explained.

His jaw was tight, but he looked down the barrel of the camera as he said it.

This is for me, Sophie knew with sudden blinding clarity. *He wants to show me that he can do it, that he's accepted my challenge.* She felt sick and elated all at once.

"You said earlier that something happened to send you off on this quest. Can I ask what that was?" Sheri asked.

Sophie was sure the other woman was holding her breath—Sophie was.

"I fell in love," Lucas said.

Sophie gasped and clapped her hands to her mouth.

"I fell in love," Lucas repeated. "And she made me want to be a better man."

The studio audience gave a murmur of appreciation, and Sheri smiled.

Sophie fell to her knees and crawled closer to the TV. Was this really happening? Was Lucas really making this ridiculous, over-the-top gesture for her?

"I guess I don't have to tell you that most of our audience thinks you're pretty fine just the way you are, Lucas," Sheri said.

Lucas shrugged modestly.

"She must be a pretty special lady," Sheri asked, obviously fishing. "How long have you been seeing each other?"

"We're not," Lucas said. The audience gasped. Sophie stared intently at his face, holding her breath. "She asked me for something I didn't think I had it in me to give. And I let her walk away."

Sheri blinked. "Let me get this straight—the love of your life rejected you?"

Lucas gave the ghost of a grin. "Yeah. She's stubborn. And she knew what she wanted."

Sheri shifted excitedly in her chair. "But you want her back?"

Lucas stared straight down the camera, and Sophie saw the hope and determination in his eyes. "I love her. I want to spend the rest of my life with her. I want her to know that she's the best thing that ever happened to me."

Tears streamed down Sophie's face. "You idiot!" she told the television screen. "You didn't need to do this. You didn't need to prove it to me beyond a doubt."

On screen, Lucas took out his cell phone and laid it on the table in front of him. Still staring down the barrel of the camera, he spoke directly to her.

"Sophie, don't make me jump on the couch," he said, a hopeful smile curling the corners of his mouth.

"Oh, my God," Sophie said. Then she scrambled for her address book to find the cell number he'd given her the day they came to Sydney.

Snatching up the phone, she realized that Becky was still on the line.

"Sophie, Sophie!" she was yelling, obviously trying to get Sophie's attention.

"I have to go," Sophie said.

"Tell me you're calling him. Because if you're not,

I am personally coming around to strangle you with my bare hands," Becky said.

"I'm calling him."

She ended the call and stabbed at the number pad with a shaking finger.

"Sophie?"

His voice sounded so good, so familiar, she burst into tears all over again.

"Lucas," she sobbed.

"Don't cry, sweetheart. I love you," he said.

Out of the corner of her eye, she saw that Lucas had vacated the chair on the Sheri Malcolm's show, and Sheri was talking direct to camera. Lucas had obviously walked off the set the moment she'd called.

"I can't believe you just did that," she said.

"I've got nothing to hide anymore, Soph. I wanted you to know it, absolutely."

"You're insane. Completely off your rocker."

"But you love me?" he asked. It killed her to hear the doubt and hope in his voice.

"Are you kidding me? I'm mad about you. I dream about you every night. I almost call you every day. I can't get you out of my head."

"I don't want you to. Are you at home?"

"Yes. But I've moved," she said.

"Rose Bay. I know. Give me twenty minutes."

He ended the call, and Sophie sat back on her haunches. Almost immediately, her phone rang again.

"Sophie." It was her mom. "Please tell me you were just watching Sheri Malcolm. I tried to call you but the line was busy."

"I saw it."

"And?"

"He loves me!" Sophie said.

"I know. I think that answers your questions, don't you think?" her mother said wisely.

"More than. Above and beyond the call of duty."

"Good. I'm very happy for you, darling."

Sophie smiled, smoothing a palm down her pyjama-clad leg. Suddenly she registered what she was wearing. And the fact that she hadn't showered this morning, or brushed her teeth, or shaved her legs for nearly a month.

"Mom, I have to go," she squeaked into the phone.

She nearly killed herself running into the bathroom and jumping beneath the shower. Working frantically, she tried to reverse four weeks of mooching around and general self-neglect.

Within five minutes she was out of the shower and dragging clean underwear on over her still-wet body. A pair of jeans and a tank top and a pair of slip-on sandals later, she slammed out the front door of her apartment to run down the steps and wait for Lucas on the street.

As she stood there, the hot Australian sun beating down on her wet hair, she closed her eyes and thought about Lucas: his smell, the warm velvet of his skin, the low timbre of his voice, the tawny heat of his eyes. He was hers. He was offering himself up to her in the way that she'd offered herself to him. Wholly. Irrevocably. Generously.

When she opened her eyes again, Lucas was climbing out of his Porsche, tall and tanned and gorgeous in a crisp white shirt and jeans. She launched herself at him, wrapping her legs around his waist and burrowing her face into his neck as she held him to her with every bit of strength she had.

"I love you, I love you, I love you," she chanted into his neck. "I have been eating my heart out over you every day. What took you so long?!"

He laughed and hugged her back so tightly that she couldn't breathe. "Sophie Gallagher, will you marry me? Will you have babies with me and teach me to cook and laugh with me and grow old and eccentric with me?"

She kissed him, her hands coursing into his hair to hold his head as she gave him her soul.

"Yes. Please," she said after a long, long time.

He kissed her back then, and things soon became pretty heated. Lucas remembered they were in a quiet suburban street before things got technically illegal, and they sprinted up the stairs two at a time and raced each other to Sophie's bedroom. Kicking off clothes with frantic abandon, they came together on the bed and held each other tight.

"Sophie. I'm so sorry I made you wait. I'm so sorry I wasn't ready for what you gave me. I'll make it up to you, I promise," he said, his hands cupping her face tenderly as he bumped noses with her.

"You already have," she said, and then he was inside her and they were making love.

Each stroke, each kiss, each sigh was a gift they gave each other, until finally they gripped each other tight as they found ecstasy. Afterward, Lucas held her and stroked her arms, her legs, her belly as he reacquainted himself with her body.

"There are things I need to tell you," he said after a

while. "About what happened. I understand now about my nightmare."

Curled up against his side, Sophie listened as he told her about the journey he'd gone on to excavate the truth of his past. It had taken him a full week to track down the people who'd been the first to take him into care. He'd flown to Queensland to talk to the social worker who'd been listed on his forms. As he'd told Sheri—and the rest of Australia—his mother, Tess, had been a young, single Englishwoman. That much he'd been able to find out from his file. The social worker had told him the rest.

Tess's landlady, an old woman named Dorothy Hobb, had taken Tess under her wing when Lucas was barely one and become quite attached to the two of them, apparently. They lived together in Dorothy's rambling old house in the leafy Sydney suburb of Paddington. When Lucas was three years old, his mother died of a burst appendix. Dorothy did her best to find relatives to take Lucas on, but had no luck with any of the letters or phone calls to England. So Dorothy did her best by him for nearly nine months until she suffered a massive stroke while posting a letter out front of her house. A passerby called an ambulance, and she died in hospital that evening, never having regained consciousness.

Sophie wrapped her body around Lucas as much as she could at this point, guessing intuitively what came next. His nightmare…

"I was alone in her house for three days before they found me," Lucas said quietly, the words a whisper against her skin. "Apparently I couldn't speak for a week, I'd been screaming for help for so long."

Sophie kissed him, wanting desperately to make up for the sadness of his childhood. She guessed there was more—he'd been in care for fourteen years, there was bound to be more. But he wasn't denying it anymore. And now that he had invited her into his life and his heart, she would show him what love could be like, what it should be like.

"I think you're amazing," she told him.

"No. I just met an amazing woman," he said.

They kissed, and Sophie put her head on his chest and threaded her fingers through his.

"You were loved, Lucas. Your mother, Dorothy. No one gave you up," she said, in case he hadn't made the connection himself.

"I know."

"And I love you so much. Maybe too much, considering how much the past four weeks have sucked. I'm yours, all yours."

He looked deep into her eyes and for the first time she saw nothing but openness and love and hope there.

"And I'm all yours," he said. "Thank you for saving me, Sophie."

She smiled tenderly. "It was my pleasure."

* * * * *

*Look for Sarah Mayberry's next
Harlequin Blaze novel!
Coming in June 2008.*

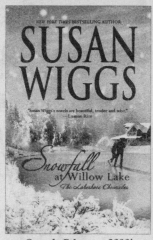

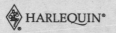

HARLEQUIN®
Blaze™

COMING NEXT MONTH

#381 GETTING LUCKY Joanne Rock
Blush

Sports agent Dex Brantley used to be the luckiest man alive. But since rumors of a family curse floated to the surface, he's been on a losing streak. To reverse that, he hooks up again with sexy psychic Lara Wyland. Before long he's lucky in a whole new way!

#382 SHAKEN AND STIRRED Kathleen O'Reilly
Those Sexy O'Sullivans, Bk. 1

When Gabe O'Sullivan describes his friend Tessa Hart as a work in progress, it gets Tessa to thinking. She's carried a torch for Gabe forever, but maybe now's the time to light the first spark and show him who's really ready to take their sexy flirting to the next level!

#383 OFF LIMITS Jordan Summers

Love happens when you least expect it. Especially on an airplane between Delaney Carter, an undercover ATF agent, and Jack Gordon, a former arms dealer. With their lives on the line, can they find a way to trust each other… once they're out of bed?

#384 BEYOND HIS CONTROL Stephanie Tyler

A reunion rescue mission turns life-threatening just as navy SEAL Justin Brandt realizes he's saving former high school flame Ava Turkowski. Talk about a blast from the past…

#385 WHAT HAPPENED IN VEGAS… Wendy Etherington

For Jacinda Barrett, leaving Las Vegas meant leaving behind her exotic dancer self. Now she's respectable…in every way. Then Gideon Nash—her weekend-she'll-never-forget hottie—shows up. Suddenly she's got the urge to lose the clothes…and the respectability!

#386 COMING SOON Jo Leigh
Do Not Disturb

Concierge Mia Traverse discovers a body in the romantic Hush hotel, which is booked for a movie shoot. Detective Bax Milligan is assigned to investigate and keep Mia under wraps. Hiding out with her in a sexy suite is perfect—except for *who* and *what* is coming next….

HBCNM0208